... 'Ah   that I
shouldn't, don't

Sara frowned. 'What do you mean?'

'It doesn't matter,' came the reply. 'What does matter, however, is your telling all our little secrets.'

'Little secrets? I don't understand.'

'People don't believe in us these days. That's why we are never caught, because people don't know how to. And then you go and give away all our secrets – wooden stakes, running water, no reflections . . .'

Sara's breath caught in her throat. She backed away, towards the door.

But it was too late.

BOOKS IN THIS SERIES
AVAILABLE FROM BOXTREE

DreaM Lover

Nigel Robinson

B⧫XTREE

First published in Great Britain in 1994 by Boxtree Limited,
Broadwall House, 21 Broadwall, London SE1 9PL

Copyright © 1994 Nigel Robinson

10 9 8 7 6 5 4 3 2 1

ISBN: 0 7522 09817

Cover art by Paul Campbell
Typeset by SX Composing Ltd., Rayleigh, Essex
Printed and bound in Great Britain by
BPC Paperbacks Ltd

A CIP catalogue entry is available from the British Library.

Chapter One

It was the night of the full moon at Castle-mare, and a huge summer moon, the colour of old parchment, dominated the cloudless sky above one of the most exclusive schools in the country. In its pale-yellow light, the stone buildings of the school looked even more ancient than they in fact were. Castle-mare was only about four hundred years old, but in this light it would have been easy to imagine that the school had been standing here for many more centuries, long before the dissolution of the monasteries, or the Great Plague, even long before William the Conqueror was crowned King of all England only a few miles away in nearby London. Castlemare belonged to another time, a time when strange unearthly creatures roamed the forests of these lands, a time when evil had dominion over those twelve long hours after dusk when good people dared not leave the shelter of their homes.

Summer breezes rustled the leaves of the

yew trees in the school grounds and, if you listened carefully enough, you could hear the frogs croaking at the edge of the lake, or grasshoppers chirping in the bushes.

And there was another sound too, a noise which only a few would recognise. *Skreek – skreek. Skreeeeek!* Their shapes flitted across the round shape of the moon, like deadly bacteria held in solution and viewed through a microscope.

Bats. The children of the night had come home to Castlemare.

And they were hungry.

Jake Allan wiped the sweat off his brow, and pushed his way through the crowd of dancers and revellers to the bar. It was the last night of the summer term, and once again the celebrating students at Castlemare High were putting on the party to end all parties.

On the dance floor serious ravers were grooving away to the heaviest house and the trendiest techno beats around. At the bar sixth-formers were ordering cups of mineral water, topping them up with the wine they'd sneaked in past the teachers on duty. In darkened corners more adventurous students were getting to know each other a little more intimately than they would have been allowed to during term-time.

What the heck? thought Jake, as he

ordered a can of Diet Coke. *It's the start of the summer vacation. We might as well start as we mean to go on!*

Jake looked around at his fellow party-goers. At one end of the bar, the attractive – *no*, Jake corrected himself, *make that heart-stoppingly gorgeous* – the heart-stoppingly gorgeous Kirsty Pemberton was in a serious snog situation with Marc Carter. When Marc noticed Jake looking at them, he gave the American boy the finger, and Jake abruptly turned away, embarrassed.

At the other end of the bar, Doug Hathaway was exercising his not inconsiderable charms on the pretty Bernadette Murphy. Bernadette caught Jake staring enviously at them and told him in her Irish brogue, and in no uncertain terms, exactly where he could get off.

'Penny for them, *amigo*?'

Jake turned around and was grateful to see the smiling face of Sandor, his best friend. Like Jake, Sandor was dripping with perspiration, despite wearing only a Calvin Klein singlet and trendy shorts. That was, however, where the similarity ended.

Jake was muscular and of average height, his dark-blond hair cut into a stylish Number Two crop which, together with his firm jaw and moodily-dark eyes, made him look like a rough 'n' sexy extra from a biker movie – *The Wild One* maybe, or *Rumble Fish*.

Sandor, on the other hand, was a Latin American smoothie, tall and slim, with long, sleek, jet-black hair which he always wore in a pony-tail. He looked like the romantic lead in a slushy and sentimental silent movie from the 1920s, the sort Jake's great-grandmother used to watch. All the girls at Castlemare positively drooled over Sandor – and he loved it.

'Once again, *amigo*, a penny for them?' Sandor repeated. 'This is the last night of term – you're supposed to be happy. You, however, look as if it's the end of the world!'

Jake took a sip of his Diet Coke and shrugged. He glanced over at Kirsty and Marc, who were moving off to the dance floor. Sandor got the message.

'Aha!' he said with a grin. 'Summer holiday blues, yes?'

Jake smiled, in spite of himself, and ordered Sandor a glass of mineral water (with white wine). 'It's going to be a long and lonely summer, my man!' he said dramatically.

'Because you're not going out with a girl at the moment?' Sandor asked.

'Because I haven't been going out with anyone for the past six months,' Jake reminded him. 'What am I supposed to do for the next three months – sit at home and watch my dad's cruddy horror videos? What's wrong with me, old buddy?'

Sandor sighed. 'So you are not going out with a girl at the moment. What is the problem? Neither am I!' He took a sip of his wine and grimaced. It was gut-rot stuff, not like the kind his father grew back home in their posh vineyards in the Mendoza region of Argentina.

'Yeah, but you could have the pick of the chicks here,' Jake pointed out accurately, and stood aside to allow a pretty fair-haired girl to get to the bar. 'But whenever I come on to a girl, they tell me that I'm a real nice guy, but that they'd much rather we just remain good mates!'

'Better to be a good mate than a boyfriend,' the fair-haired girl said fliply, and ordered two mineral waters (without wine) from the bar. 'We girls get through boyfriends like used Kleenexes. Once we've got what we want from them, we drop 'em. Good mates we keep forever!'

'Thank you very much for those words of comfort, Vicky,' Jake said sarcastically. 'They don't help very much at the moment!' He looked over enviously at Doug and Bernadette, who were indulging in a pretty heavy clinch. It looked as though they were two people who weren't going to be lonely during the forthcoming vacation.

'I mean, what's wrong with me?' Jake asked Sandor and Vicky. 'Seventeen years old and no steady girlfriend!'

'I don't have a girlfriend,' Sandor reminded him once again. 'And there's nothing wrong with me!'

'And I don't have a boyfriend,' Vicky said, flicking back her short blonde hair. 'And if you even dare say there's something wrong with me, Jake Allan, I'll hit you where it really hurts and put an end to your chances of scoring with a girl ever again!'

Jake raised his hands good-naturedly and smiled. 'OK, point taken!' he said. He indicated Vicky's two cups of mineral water.

'One's for Kim,' she said. Kim Nishida, the pretty Japanese student, waved at her friend from across the dance floor, where she was bopping with a handsome Italian boy.

Vicky turned to Jake. 'Stop taking things so seriously,' she advised. 'And stop looking around for a girlfriend.'

'And if I do, do you think one will find me?'

'Maybe,' Vicky said with a smile. 'Besides, you haven't exactly been on the market this term, have you?'

'What d'you mean?' Jake asked.

'You've been working so hard, shutting yourself up in the lab until the caretaker throws you out,' she reminded him. 'You're not going to meet any potential girlfriends over a rusty old Bunsen burner!'

Jake laughed. 'When I leave Castlemare I want to become a medical student,' he said. 'I need to put in the long hours.'

Sandor pulled a face and looked over at Vicky. 'I met him in the lab once,' he told her. 'He was doing experiments on all these test tubes filled with blood! He looked like a character from one of those horror films his dad makes.'

'Yuk!' Vicky joined in the joke. 'Vampire city!'

Jake bared his teeth at Vicky, like he'd seen Bela Lugosi do in *Dracula*, one of his dad's favourite movies. 'I was researching blood substitutes – y'know, plasma. Our hospitals are running out of blood for transfusions. If we can fabricate some sort of effective substitute, then the benefits could be enormous.'

'And you, of course, are going to be the person who does it?' asked Vicky.

'Why not?' Jake said. 'Castlemare has never produced a Nobel-Prize-winning scientist yet. Who knows? I could be the first!'

Jake held out his left arm for Vicky and Sandor to inspect. He pointed at his veins, which were blue and prominent on his white, muscular arm. 'There you go,' he said proudly. 'AB!'

Sandor and Vicky exchanged blank looks. 'Blood group AB!' Jake continued. 'The rarest blood group in the world. Only about three per cent of people share my blood!'

'And I'm supposed to be impressed by that?' Vicky asked jokingly.

'Well, how many guys have you been out with who possess the rarest blood in the world?' Jake asked.

'It might surprise you to know, Jake, but I don't ask to see a boy's medical records before I decide whether or not I want to go out with him,' Vicky said. 'It's all the same to me what sort of blood they have – as long as it's suitably blue, of course.' She winked mischievously at them and took Kim her cup of water, before rejoining her own dancing partner, a slightly nerdy and aristocratic-looking boy called Clive.

Jake sighed and turned to Sandor. 'Sheesh!' he moaned. 'What has that nerd Clive got that I haven't?'

Sandor laughed. 'A double-barrelled name and a title perhaps?' he suggested. 'You know that history is Vicky's big thing. She's fascinated by all those aristocratic families. Of course, Clive is also remarkably wealthy . . .'

'So a poor little guy from Sacramento is going to have no chance with a snob like her then?' Jake asked.

Sandor slapped his friend on the back. 'Vicky's no snob and you know it,' he said.

'And you're hardly a poor little guy from Sacramento, my friend. Your dad is one of the top movie directors in the world!'

'You think if I promised one of the girls a lead in his next film, they'd go out with me?' Jake asked hopefully. 'Maybe if I showed them around the set – I've got Access All Areas down at the film studios.'

Sandor smiled and shook his head. 'The movie he's working on at the moment is called *The House on Hell Drive . . .*'

'Not romantic enough, huh?'

'Hardly,' agreed Sandor, catching the eye of a particularly sexy redhead who had just entered the hall. 'Jake, I'll catch you later, OK?' he said. 'Someone very important has just walked in the room!' And with that Sandor marched off to greet the redhead just as if they were old friends, when in fact they had never met before.

Jake watched his best mate going through his normal chat-up line and then turned philosophically to the girl behind the bar.

'He sure doesn't waste much time,' the girl smiled, offering Jake another Diet Coke. 'On the house,' she said and waved aside the money that Jake passed to her. 'Old Mother Greystone won't notice one can more or less – and I can't stand a man looking as down in the dumps as you are!'

'Thanks, Sara,' Jake said, resting his chin

on his hand. 'I'm looking real miserable, am I?'

Sara nodded. 'Cheer up, Jake, it might never happen,' she chirped cheerily.

'That's what I'm worried about,' he said, and Sara laughed. With her long auburn hair, green cat's eyes and stylishly grungy clothes, Sara looked like the subject of a Pre-Raphaelite painting. Although not as beautiful as some of the more glamorous girls at Castlemare, she was an extremely popular student and everybody's best friend.

'I don't suppose you know any girl who'd like a personally conducted tour of *The House on Hell Drive*, do you, Sara?' Jake asked hopefully. Sara giggled and shook her head.

'Damn him!' Jake said. 'Other kids' dads are working on slushy romantic films, with some of the sexiest names in the business. Why do I have to end up with a father who produces tacky low-budget horror movies?'

'I love horror movies,' said a gentle voice behind him. Jake turned around.

A beautiful girl was standing next to him. She was about Jake's height and was dressed in a long black cape, which covered a red silk dress that reached down almost to the ground. Her jet-black hair was worn loose and long, and there was a single streak of grey running through it. She smiled at him and revealed dazzlingly white teeth.

10

'I used to love watching them on TV in my home country,' she continued. She spoke English well, but there was a certain foreign burr in her warm voice. Jake tried to place it. Germany? One of the Eastern European countries?

'Well, you might have seen some of my dad's films then,' said Jake, enthusiastically reeling off a list of some of the better-known ones. The newcomer shook her head, which proved to Jake that here was one classy girl at least.

'My name is Rebecca Vondertoten,' the girl said. Jake told her his name and offered her a glass of red wine. Rebecca refused. 'I never drink. Well at least, not wine,' she said.

'Then how about a Perrier?' Jake suggested.

'That will be splendid,' Rebecca said.

Jake ordered the bottle of mineral water from Sara, who then discreetly moved further on down the bar so that Jake and Rebecca could talk in private. Jake watched as Rebecca poured the water into a plastic cup and sipped delicately at it, all the time watching him through dark, narrowed eyes over the rim of the cup.

'I haven't seen you here before,' Jake said. *And I'd sure have noticed someone as sexy as you!* he thought. Jake marvelled at his own

11

audacity and made a mental note to start using more of Sandor's standard chat-up lines. 'Are you a student here?'

'I will be next term,' Rebecca replied. 'I have just moved to this country. Miss Greystone, the Principal, has allowed me to come to the dance tonight so that I can meet some of my fellow students.' She looked around at the crowd of dancers on the dance floor. 'It is all so busy and different from my own home,' she said with wonder.

'And where is home?' asked Jake, moving closer to Rebecca. *This is amazing! The most exciting and sexy girl in the whole school — and she's only got eyes for me! Jake, my man, your luck has suddenly changed!*

Rebecca sighed. 'I come from a country a long, long way from here,' she said mysteriously. 'But now I live here with my aunt in the old house on Hobb Hill.'

'Hey, you don't mean that tumbledown Gothic folly on the other side of the Heath?' Jake asked. Rebecca nodded. 'Wow, but like that place is real *Addams Family*,' the American boy continued. 'My dad wanted to use it for some of the exterior scenes for his new movie, but the dotty old bag who owns the house told him he couldn't . . .' Jake's voice tailed off as he suddenly realised what he had said. He smacked his forehead with the palm of his hand. 'Shoot! Me and my big mouth again!'

Rather than being annoyed, Rebecca started to chuckle. 'That's right, Jake,' she said, wagging a mock-reproving finger at him. 'That "dotty old bag" is my aunt.'

'Sorry . . .' *Darn it! Now I've gone and completely screwed up my chances with her!*

'You need not be sorry,' Rebecca reassured him. 'Sometimes my aunt gives the impression of being a little – how shall we say? – eccentric. But she is really a very sweet and caring old lady.' Rebecca turned away for a second. 'Sometimes,' she murmured, in a voice too soft for Jake to hear.

'Look, I wonder if you'd like to dance,' Jake said.

Rebecca smiled and slipped off her cloak, handing it to Sara behind the bar. 'I'd love to,' she said, and took Jake's hand and led him out on to the dance floor.

Rebecca danced well, as lithely as a cat, and Jake suddenly found himself the envy of all the other boys on the floor. His heart swelled with pride, as he realised that of all the good-looking and sexy boys in the hall this beautiful foreign beauty had chosen to zero in on him. They danced for almost an hour, and when they returned to the bar, Jake was shining with sweat. Rebecca, however, was as cool and composed as she had been when they started dancing. There was not a trace of perspiration on her aristocratic brow. She ordered two more mineral waters from Sara and then smiled at Jake.

'Thank you, Jake,' she said. 'It isn't very often that I'm allowed to go out. I haven't enjoyed myself so much for a long, long time.'

Jake beamed at her. 'Hey, no problem,' he said. 'I enjoyed myself too!'

'I must thank you properly,' Rebecca said, and pressed her mouth onto Jake's lips. The force of her kiss almost took Jake's breath away: he'd been kissed by several girls in the past, but by none as expert as this one!

When they finally came up for air, Jake stammered his thanks.

'It is the least I can do,' Rebecca said, winking knowingly at him. 'You're a good dancer and a very nice person, Jake. I knew that from the moment I walked in here.'

'I'm flattered,' Jake said. 'There are loads of good-looking guys here.'

'Aha!' said Rebecca and tapped the side of her temple. 'But I have – what should we call it? – a sort of radar which always picks out the boy who is best suited to me!'

Just then Sandor returned to the bar, his arm wrapped around the waist of the sexy redhead he'd just met. He ordered two drinks from Sara and then looked down along the bar at Jake and Rebecca. They were obviously getting on very well indeed.

Sandor whistled appreciatively to himself. 'Who's the newcomer?' he asked Sara.

Sara shrugged and handed Sandor his drinks. 'How am I supposed to know?' she said sharply. She and Sandor were hardly enemies, but neither were they the best of friends. Sara particularly disliked the way the Argentinian went out with as many girls as possible without ever committing himself to one.

'That's half the fun of working behind a bar,' Sandor said. 'You get to hear all the juicy gossip!'

'I've never seen her before,' Sara told him. 'I didn't even see her come in. It was almost as if she appeared out of thin air.'

'Whoever she is, Jake is obviously enjoying himself,' Sandor said, glad that his friend had snapped out of his previous morose mood. 'Look at him – he can't keep his eyes off her!'

Sara looked down the bar. Sandor was right. Jake was hanging eagerly onto Rebecca's every word, his head moving up and down like the nodding dog her dad kept in the back of the family car. It would be funny, she told herself, if it wasn't so pathetic! A grown boy behaving like that in front of the sexiest, most attractive girl at the party. *Men!* she thought grumpily. *They're all the same!*

'It looks like old Jake is falling in love with the mysterious lady,' Sandor said, and giggled – the wine was going to his head. 'Although what she sees in him, when she could be going out with me . . .'

The redhead on Sandor's arm wisely chose to ignore that comment, but not Sara.

'Don't you dare try and steal her from Jake,' she warned him. 'He deserves a bit of happiness!'

Sandor shook his head. 'Jake's my best friend,' he stated, suddenly serious. 'I wouldn't do that to him.' He pointed towards the door. 'And it looks as though I won't have to, anyway.'

They all turned to see the newcomer. He was about eighteen years old, tall and muscular, wearing leather trousers, biker boots and a studded leather jacket. His peroxide-blond hair was cut in a spiky-punk style, and there were dark shadows beneath his brilliantly blue eyes. He saw Rebecca and Jake, and smiled to himself – a thick, cruel smile – before swaggering over to them.

'Well, well, well,' he sneered. 'I thought I would find you here, dear Rebecca.'

Rebecca glared at the punk, and then back to Jake. There was a strange look in her eyes, Jake noticed. Fear? Despair? Or just anger that the newcomer had interrupted their conversation? Jake wasn't sure.

The punk turned his attentions not to Rebecca, but to Jake. He considered the young American, looking him up and down, as though he were sizing up a particularly succulent piece of meat. He licked his lips.

'And you are?' he asked.

'This is Jake,' Rebecca said frostily. 'And I'd ask you to keep out of my affairs, Karl.'

Karl held out his hand to Jake. 'I'm glad to know you, Jake,' he said. 'Any friend of Rebecca's is a friend of mine.' Jake accepted the young punk's proffered handshake: it felt cold and clammy to the touch, like the marble headstone his dad had bought for his mother's grave.

Rebecca glared at Karl. 'What are you doing here?' she demanded.

'Why, I've come to take you home,' he told her, but still continued to regard Jake. 'It's nearly midnight, and pretty girls like you should get their beauty sleep.'

Jake decided that he didn't like Karl's tone, nor the way in which he took Rebecca's hand and started to drag her away, apparently against her will.

'Hey, look here,' he said, 'Rebecca's only been here for an hour. Maybe she doesn't want to leave the party just yet. What right do you have to say when she comes and goes?'

'What right?' scoffed Karl. 'I have every right!'

Jake clenched his fists and took a

17

threatening step towards Karl. Just then he felt a restraining hand on his shoulder. Sandor, who had been watching everything, had walked up to them.

'Steady, *amigo*,' he soothed. 'Take it easy.'

'It's all right, Jake,' Rebecca said sadly, averting her eyes so as not to look at him.

'You sure you're OK?' Jake asked. He didn't trust Karl one little bit.

Rebecca nodded. 'I'll be fine,' she reassured him, even though she was finding it difficult to keep her lower lip from trembling. 'Karl is my . . . brother – he'll take me home.'

'Your brother?' Jake asked in disbelief, and Rebecca nodded. Jake looked from Rebecca to Karl and back again: there was absolutely nothing to suggest they were brother and sister. Rebecca's eyes were narrow and dark; Karl's wide and bright. The punk's mouth was cruel and twisted; Rebecca's lips were full and inviting.

'That's right, I'm her brother,' Karl sneered. He stared at Jake – a long, appraising stare. 'And we live with our aunt on Hobb Hill.'

Jake looked at Rebecca again. 'You're certain you want to go now?' he asked. 'You'll miss the midnight feast.'

'Midnight feast?' Rebecca repeated, intrigued.

'Yeah,' said Jake. 'It's an idea of Miss

Greystone's. At midnight on the last night of term all the teachers come and serve us a midnight buffet.' He sniggered. 'I guess it's their way of making up for being so goddamn awful to us for the rest of the term!'

Rebecca's eyes suddenly sparkled. 'I'd love to stay with you for the midnight feast, Jake,' she said, and then looked at her brother. He was shaking his head.

'If you stay we'll be late home, and we both know how angry Aunt can be if we stay out late,' Karl said. 'We can always grab a takeaway on the way home. What do you fancy – Indian or Chinese?'

Sara, who had been half-listening to the conversation, interrupted. 'Tokyo Joe's is still open,' she said, referring to the trendy Japanese bistro that was frequented by many of the Castlemare students.

Karl grinned. 'Japanese it is then,' he said, licking his lips. 'Now that is unusual. What do you say, sister dear?'

Rebecca hung her head. 'Whatever you say, *brother*.' She looked up at Jake. 'I have to go now,' she said. 'It was so nice meeting you.'

'You're sure you're OK?' Jake asked. 'My car's outside and I haven't been drinking any alcohol. I can drive you home later if you like, after the feast.'

Rebecca looked back at Karl, who again

shook her head. She turned back to Jake. 'Thanks, Jake, but Karl will give me a lift home on his motorbike.' She started to walk away. 'I had a really good time with you tonight, Jake,' she said.

'Hey, can we see each other again?' Jake asked. 'Maybe during the vacation?'

Karl grinned. 'I'm sure Rebecca will see you again, Jake,' he said, and chuckled. 'After all, you know where we live.'

Rebecca glared at her brother. 'You're a wonderful boy, Jake,' she breathed. 'I'm sure you'll find a nice girl one day . . . Goodbye.'

Rebecca turned and walked smartly out of the door. Karl paused for a moment and winked knowingly at Jake, Sandor and Sara, before following his sister. Seconds later all three of them heard the revving of the punk's motorbike as he and his sister drove off into the night.

'Well, what do you make of that?' asked Sara. 'Weird, or what?'

'She was beautiful,' Jake said. 'And we were getting on so well until that creep arrived.'

Sandor laid a sympathetic hand on his best mate's shoulder. 'Hey, you know what brothers are like, *amigo*,' he said. 'They're always so protective of their sisters. I know that I'd behave just like him if someone was trying to chat up my sister.'

'Your sister is two years old, Sandor,' Sara pointed out.

'*De nada*,' Sandor shrugged, and then grinned. 'It is the same principle.'

'Besides, they weren't brother and sister,' Jake said firmly.

'What?'

'Whatever their relationship, they're not brother and sister,' he repeated.

'You mean that they are boyfriend and girlfriend?' Sandor asked.

'I don't know,' admitted Jake. 'But did you see the way she looked at him? Like . . . like she was scared. Like she was scared for her life!'

Chapter Two

Kim Nishida walked swiftly along the path to her parents' home, on the far side of London's Hampstead Heath. Her parents had often warned her about taking this short cut across the middle of the Heath, but Kim never listened. After all, she was an expert at karate, having learnt it at home in Honshu, the largest of Japan's islands. She had reached the fourth *kyu*, or grade, and had earned the right to wear the coveted orange belt. She'd like to see any mugger try to attack her, on Hampstead Heath or anywhere else in the world!

She looked up at the full moon, and smiled. Kim liked the moon, regarding it as a friend rather than a lump of rock hanging up there in space. Its blue light shone out a path for her amongst the undergrowth and twisted tree roots of the Heath. She could see her shadow, silhouetted against the moonbeams.

To her right Kim could see the lights of

Castlemare, where the party was still going strong, and much further off the neons of London, hazy and twinkling in the summer smog. Kim chuckled. There were some at Castlemare who said she was crazy for preferring the light of the moon to the glare of the nightclubs in the West End. But the moon up in the sky was the same moon her ancestors in Japan had worshipped, the same moon that had shone over the forests of Europe in the primeval night. Even in this modern age of computers and spaceships, Kim realised that you couldn't escape the past, the old powers that had been part of life on this planet since history began. Kim rather liked that.

The summer breeze sighed in the leaves of the trees, as Kim made her way along the path. From far off, she could hear the sound of dogs barking: probably some of the residents of the posh houses on the edge of the Heath, taking their pet mutts out for a final late-night run.

Skreek. Skreek. Skreeeeek.

Kim frowned and looked up in the direction of the noise, which had come from the highest branches of a towering old beech tree. She shuddered. It was illogical, she knew, but she hated bats. *Flying vermin*, her father had once called them, and she agreed with him. Kim pulled her coat more tightly around her and increased her pace. She glanced at her Swatch: 11.54. It would soon be midnight, and if she didn't hurry, she'd miss that TV movie that she'd forgotten to set the VCR for.

Suddenly something threw itself into her face, and Kim instinctively raised her hands to defend herself. Her hands hit something small and furry, which let out a shriek of pained surprise and then flew off.

Damn these bats! she thought angrily, and hurried along the path.

Perhaps alerted by its fellow, several more bats swooped out of the tree and hovered around Kim's head. She looked up nervously. The bats weren't attacking her — they were toying with her, tormenting her, playing with her as a cat plays with a mouse. She reached into her jacket pockets and took out her beret, which she rammed down on top of her head, covering her long dark hair. The last thing she wanted was for one of these blasted creatures to dive down and get entangled in her hair.

There was a rustling noise in the bushes lining the footpath. Kim turned to see two eyes glinting in the moonlight. The eyes slowly approached Kim, and she could hear the creature which they belonged to growl. The dogs were no longer barking in the distance, and even the bats had veered away from Kim and where chirruping nervously among themselves.

'Wh-who's there?' Kim asked. 'Would someone please help me?' No reply. Still the creature kept under cover of the bushes, revealing nothing of itself other than its eyes.

Where's the dog's owner? Kim asked herself angrily. *Don't people know they shouldn't let their dogs out at night unaccompanied?* But something deep down inside Kim told her that the creature in the undergrowth was much more than a mere dog.

Kim heard a wet, sucking sound, as if the creature were licking its lips, slavering over her pale and succulent flesh. She remembered something she had read a long time ago, that animals will never attack you if you show that you're not afraid. She began to move away, slowly, trying desperately to hide her fear.

'E-e-easy, boy,' she whispered, in a sing-song voice. 'I'm not going to hurt you.' She kept her eyes fixed on those of the creature, those eyes which blazed savagely in the moonlight.

Suddenly the creature threw back its head and howled at the moon. It was a noise that might have come from hell itself.

Something inside Kim snapped. She turned round and ran off down the path. With an angry snarl the creature sprang out of the bushes and darted after her. Kim could feel its hot breath on her heels, smell its fetid stink as it bore down on her.

With muscles aching, and her heart ready to burst out of her chest, Kim shut out the pain that was coursing through her body. She didn't dare look behind and, in her fear, didn't wonder why whatever was pursuing her hadn't caught up with her yet. It was snapping at her feet, but wasn't biting her – as if, like the bats, it was playing with her, or leading her somewhere.

In the distance Kim saw the street lamps which fringed the Heath, and beyond that the ramshackle yet threatening silhouette of the old house on top of Hobb Hill. There was a light showing in one of the windows but, as soon as Kim noticed it, it went out.

For God's sake, someone help me! she heard herself praying, as the air cut through her lungs like a knife. And then, as if in answer to her prayer, she heard the purring of a motorbike and saw its headlight before her as it puttered down a path which crossed hers.

'Stop! Please stop!' she cried. 'For pity's sake, please help me.'

The motorbike squealed to a halt, and Kim ran down the path towards it, throwing herself into the arms of the biker.

'Thank God you're here!' she sobbed, and

27

looked up at the stranger. He was wearing a studded leather jacket, and his peroxide-blond hair shone strangely in the moonlight. His eyes were a brilliant blue. He looked strangely familiar: hadn't she caught a glimpse of him at the party earlier on, chatting with Jake and Sandor? Perhaps he was one of their mates from the local comp down the road?

The biker made no attempt to push Kim away from him, but continued to hold her in his arms. He ran his hand down the small of her back, reassuringly.

'Hey, it's OK now,' he said softly. 'What's the problem?'

Kim turned her face away from the biker and looked down the path. There was nothing there, just the usual friendly trees and bushes of Hampstead Heath, rustling in the breeze.

She looked back up at the biker. 'Something was chasing me,' she insisted. 'A dog . . .'

The biker smiled down at Kim. 'Well, there's nothing there now,' he said. 'Are you sure you didn't imagine it?'

Kim pulled herself away from the biker, her fear suddenly forgotten now that he was challenging her story.

'There *was* something there!' she said firmly. 'A big dog. Or a wolf . . .'

The biker sniggered, and for the first time Kim noticed just what a cruel and mocking smile he had. 'A wolf on Hampstead Heath? That's hardly likely, is it?' he asked. His tone was patronising, superior. 'Did you actually see this "wolf"?'

'Yes,' said Kim, and then corrected herself. 'Well, no, not exactly. I saw its eyes, in the bushes. I heard it howl. It came after me . . . like the bats did . . .'

'Bats?' The stranger laughed. 'You're from Castlemare, aren't you?' he asked.

Kim nodded. 'That's right, but I don't see what that's got to do with anything.'

'You're having a party down there tonight,' he said. 'I should know – you're keeping half the neighbourhood awake! So maybe you had a bit too much to drink, and you imagined it all . . .'

'I did not imagine it!' Kim snapped. 'There was a wolf. And the bats did attack me!'

'Maybe you've been watching too many late-night horror movies?' came another softer and familiar voice from behind Kim. She turned and tried to see who was speaking, but the figure before her was hazy, as if shrouded in mist.

And that's crazy, Kim told herself. *Whoever heard of mist in the middle of summer?*

'Or then again,' said the biker and grinned, revealing his perfectly formed white teeth which sparkled like silver in the moonlight, 'maybe you didn't imagine it at all. Maybe it did all happen. And maybe this is your very own late-night horror movie!'

Kim didn't have time to scream. She felt a pair of razor-sharp teeth plunge savagely into her neck, ripping away at her flesh. A fountain of red gushed from her jugular vein, staining her brand-new white designer blouse a deadly shade of red, and splattering the biker and his companion with her life-blood.

In the sky above the bats whirled, *skreeked* excitedly as they saw Kim thud to the ground and gloated as her attacker fell greedily on to her warm body, frantically lapping up the blood from her wounds, like a dying man desperately trying to slake his thirst.

And there was another sound too, a noise which provided a terrible counterpoint to that of Kim's life being sucked mercilessly out of her body.

It was the stomach-turning noise of some-one retching, spewing up at the horror of what they were witnessing.

And then the unmistakeable sound of someone crying: 'Not again. Why does it always have to happen again?'

Chapter Three

'I think I'm going to be sick,' said Vicky, and sat down at one of the tables in Tokyo Joe's. Even though Castlemare was now on holiday for the summer, the news of Kim's savage death had spread like wildfire amongst the students, most of whom lived on or near the Heath. Sandor smiled weakly, brought over two mugs of steaming Japanese tea and sat down beside her.

'It was Jake who found the body,' he told her, 'when he was taking his early-morning jog on the Heath this morning.'

'I know,' Vicky said. 'The police have already spoken to me – she was one of my friends after all.'

'Did they give you a hard time?' Sandor asked. Everyone knew how some members of the local police force felt about the rich kids at Castlemare High, and how they begrudged them their privileged life.

Vicky shook her head. 'They were really

kind to me,' she said. 'Even Detective Sergeant Ashby.'

'I think they're as shocked by the ferocity of the attack as everyone at Castlemare,' Sandor said.

'But who would do such a terrible thing to Kim?' Vicky asked. 'She hadn't an enemy in the world. Everyone liked her.'

Sandor shrugged. 'It's a terrible world,' he said philosophically. 'There are a lot of nutters around . . .'

'But Kim should have been able to defend herself,' Vicky said. 'She had an orange belt in karate, for goodness' sake! A nutter wouldn't have had a chance with her!'

Sandor laid a hand on Vicky's. 'Calm down,' he urged. He nodded over to the door of the restaurant, which had just opened. 'Here's Jake. Perhaps he'll be able to tell us something.'

Jake walked over to them and sat down. His face was pale and drawn, and the red rings around his eyes made it clear that he had been crying. It was five o'clock in the afternoon and he had been talking to the police since early that morning when he had discovered Kim's body.

Sandor ordered him a cup of warm *sake* from the bar. Jake normally didn't touch alcohol, but these were exceptional circumstances. He sipped gratefully on the hot rice wine.

'*Come estas*? How are you feeling now?' Sandor asked.

Jake attempted a brave smile, and failed. The memory of this morning was still too clear.

'The police say it was a motiveless murder,' he told them. 'They're going to set up a murder investigation, but privately they don't hold out much hope of catching the killer. They say senseless killings like this happen more often than most people realise.'

'But they must have some clues,' Vicky insisted.

'There were some tyre tracks on the path near where I found Kim's body,' Jake revealed.

'Tyre tracks?' asked Sandor. 'You mean a car?'

Jake shook his head. 'No,' he said. 'Sergeant Ashby reckons a motorbike . . .'.

Sandor frowned. *A motorbike.* He remembered the blond-haired punk who had gatecrashed the party last night. 'Well, surely that's something?' he suggested hopefully.

'Do you realise how many motorbikes are ridden up and down that pathway?' Jake said. 'Practically everyone at Castlemare who's got a pair of wheels uses that path as a short-cut to school. There was one strange thing though . . .'

'What was that?' asked Vicky.

'There was a pool of vomit near the motor-bike tracks. Someone had thrown up.'

'I'm not surprised,' said Sandor, who was starting to feel his own stomach heave.

'Think about it,' said Jake. 'Can you imagine a nutter killing Kim, and then throwing up afterwards? It just doesn't make sense.'

'What d'you mean?' asked Vicky, fascinated and at the same time more than a little dismayed at the direction the conversation was taking.

'Well, butchers don't throw up when they slaughter a cow, do they?' Jake said.

Sandor wasn't convinced. 'I think that I would if I'd knifed someone,' he said.

'Kim wasn't knifed,' Jake told him flatly.

'What?'

'I found the body, remember,' he reminded his friends. 'And she certainly wasn't knifed.'

'Then how? . . .' asked Vicky.

Jake shuddered: the memory was still fresh in his mind, as fresh as Kim's seventeen-year-old blood that had stained the green heathland a deep and deadly scarlet.

'Her whole neck was ripped apart,' he told them. 'And most of her upper body as well. It was as though she had been attacked by a wild animal.'

34

'A wild animal?' Vicky asked. 'I've heard rumours about a pack of wild dogs running loose on the Heath . . .'

'This wasn't a dog,' Jake maintained. 'The police told me that Kim's wounds weren't what they'd expect from canine teeth. And another thing, too . . .'

Sandor and Vicky looked at each other, uncertain whether they wanted to hear what Jake had to tell them. Nevertheless, they urged him to continue.

'Her body was drained,' he said. 'There wasn't a trace of blood left in her. It was as though someone had drunk all her blood.'

A sudden chill seemed to descend on the room. Jake, Vicky and Sandor exchanged glances, none of them daring to pronounce the word each of them was thinking: *Vampires.*

Just then the door to the restaurant opened and a familiar figure sauntered over to the bar. It was Karl, the surly punk they had met last night. When he saw them, he started, but he quickly recovered his composure.

Vicky shivered. 'He gives me the creeps,' she said.

'He's a nasty piece of work, that's for sure,' Jake agreed.

Karl had ordered a drink and was staring at them over the rim of his glass, unblinking, just as his sister had done the previous night. Jake would have expected the punk to be drinking a bottle of trendy lager, but instead he was drinking tomato juice, the colour of warm blood. Karl licked his lips and smiled at Jake and the others.

Sandor stood up. 'Let's get out of here,' he said. 'I can't stand the way he keeps looking at us.' Vicky and Jake followed him, and as they passed Karl, Vicky stopped and glared at the punk.

'Have you got a problem?' she demanded, despite Jake and Sandor telling her to leave the boy alone.

Karl put down his glass and smiled. The glass had left a ring of tomato juice on his surly lips. *Like blood,* thought Jake once again.

'A problem?' Karl asked.

'Yeah, you've been staring at us ever since you walked in here,' Vicky said.

'How could I not look at such a beautiful girl like yourself?' Karl asked. He reached out his hand to her neck. 'Such a fine and graceful neck too, like a swan's...'

Vicky pushed his hand away. 'Get lost, creep!' she said.

Karl sulked, picked up his glass and drank from it. His brilliantly blue eyes betrayed no emotion whatsoever, apart from a supercilious amusement.

Like he's playing a game with us! Vicky thought.

36

'I think you owe Vicky an apology,' Jake said.

'*Si*,' Sandor agreed.

Karl bowed his head. 'Then I apologise unreservedly, if I have upset the fair lady,' he said, in a curiously formal tone of voice. He turned quickly to Jake, and his voice changed to a hiss. 'As you should have done last night to my sister!'

'Rebecca?'

'You have upset my sister,' Karl stated. 'You have awoken emotions in her that a young girl her age should not experience.'

Jake looked at Sandor, and then back at Karl. What was he going on about? And why was he putting on that sort of old-fashioned language you normally only found in a Jane Austen novel, the kind of stuff people used to come out with a hundred years ago.

'You must not see my sister ever again, Jacob Allan,' Karl said.

'Surely she should make that decision?' Jake said, annoyed at Karl's superior manner. 'She's over sixteen, and I guess she can make her own mind up. She doesn't need a minder like you.'

Karl slammed his glass down on the bar, and made a move towards Jake. 'I warn you . . .' he began, but Sandor stepped forward and cut him short.

'Your sister seemed to be enjoying herself

plenty last night with Jake,' he said. 'Maybe she should decide what is good for her!'

'My sister does not know what is good for her!' Karl spat back. He glared at Sandor, almost as if defying the young Argentinian to strike him. Then he growled and pushed his way past Sandor, Jake and Vicky, and left the restaurant, slamming the door shut behind him. A few seconds later they heard his motorbike roar into action, and he sped off down the road towards Hobb Hill.

Jake whistled in amazement. 'Do you believe that guy?' he asked his two friends. 'What planet does he come from? Is he over-protective or what?'

'He *is* possessive,' Sandor said. 'He reminds me of some of the men back home in my own country. They are so macho, and believe that all women are their personal property – that they, as men, know what is best for them.'

'Which, of course, you do not, Sandor?' Vicky asked in an effort to lighten the atmosphere.

'Ah, but I alone of all the men in this world truly know what is best for all women,' Sandor said, jokingly. 'It is that they should all go out with me!'

Vicky joined in the joke, but Jake's face remained serious. There was a dark look on his brow.

38

'What is wrong, *amigo*?' Sandor asked.

'Karl has a motorbike,' Jake said slowly.

'*Si*, but I don't see how . . .' Sandor began, and then realised what Jake was trying to say. 'Now, you're not seriously suggesting that . . .'

'He could have followed Kim last night,' Jake said.

Sandor shook his head. 'And so could many other people, Jake,' he said. 'Remember what you said yourself. Practically everyone at Castlemare who owns a motorbike uses the path where Kim was found.'

Jake shrugged. 'Maybe you're right, Sandor. I'm letting my imagination run riot,' he admitted, and both Sandor and Vicky agreed. 'But there's something else too. Remember what he said when he came to pick up Rebecca?'

'To be perfectly honest, I wasn't paying too much attention at the time,' Sandor said, reminding them of the attractive redhead he had been with.

'He suggested that he and Rebecca grab a takeaway on the way home. And then he laughed when they decided to go for a *Japanese* . . .'

Vicky thought of laughing herself at Jake's preposterous comment, until she realised he was in deadly earnest.

'Karl's got something to do with Kim's murder, I'm sure of it!' Jake said.

'And you're sure of this because of a strange throwaway remark he made last night, and the fact that he's an obnoxious creep on a motorbike?' asked Sandor, shaking his head sadly. 'It's not much to build a case on, *amigo*.'

'I've a funny feeling about him, that's all,' Jake said, not very convincingly.

'Oh, great,' Vicky scoffed. 'That's all we need – a hunch!'

'And then there's Rebecca too,' Jake said.

'Aha, *la bella* Rebecca.' Here, at last, was something Sandor could relate to.

'You saw how she reacted last night when Karl came for her,' Jake reminded him. 'She was terrified – scared for her life! He's got her under some sort of power, I know it!'

Sandor put his hand on Jake's shoulder. 'My friend, you are under a lot of stress at the moment,' he said. Jake shook his hand off his shoulder.

'Rebecca's in trouble, and Karl's the cause of it!' he declared. 'And I'm going to help her!' And with that, Jake stormed out of Tokyo Joe's.

As soon as Jake had gone, Vicky let out a sigh. 'What's got into him, Sandor?' she asked. 'It's as though he's suddenly turned crazy.'

Sandor smiled and ordered a lager from the bar. 'I think Jake has just realised that he has fallen in love,' he said sadly. 'And that is the craziest thing of all.'

Chapter Four

The sun was setting below the trees of Hampstead Heath as Jake drove his battered old Metro up the winding lanes of Hobb Hill to the house at its very top. Bathed in the light of the dying sun, it took on a threatening appearance, reminding Jake of the time he had gone on safari with his father to Africa. There, as dusk stalked quickly across the plains, they had come across the body of a dying gazelle. Perched on a rock above the animal's carcass was a vulture, patiently waiting for the gazelle to die so that it could feed on its still warm flesh and drink its sweet blood. That was what the house on Hobb Hill reminded him of – a giant vulture, just waiting for the right moment to swoop down on its helpless prey.

The house was set in its own grounds and surrounded by a high stone wall. It had been built in the early nineteenth century, when this area of London was still a village and to live here was the equivalent of having a country seat. Now the house was surrounded by modern apartment blocks and bijou residences. It looked oddly out of place, a disturbing anachronism in the late twentieth century.

Unlike the other buildings on the hill, it didn't have a name or, as far as Jake was aware, even a number. For miles around people knew it simply as 'the house on Hobb Hill'. It reminded Jake of the title of his dad's new horror film – *The House on Hell Drive*.

He parked his car and walked over to the rusty iron gates set in the outside wall. To his surprise they weren't locked, and he opened them and walked down the drive to the house.

On either side of the path yew trees swayed and creaked in the early-evening breeze. He gulped, remembering what Sara, who knew about these things, had mentioned to him once: the yew tree was known to the ancients as the tree of death. It was supposedly a tree of ill omen. That was why so many of them had been planted in graveyards.

Hey, stop letting your imagination run away with you, Jake, my man! he rebuked himself. *This is real life we're talking about here, not an episode of The Addams Family!*

He looked up at the fading Gothic splendour of the house on Hobb Hill, with its turrets and ornate stained-glass windows. *It looks like you were right first time, Jake!* he revised his opinion. *We are most certainly talking about an episode of The Addams Family!*

The house was in darkness. An old-fashioned limousine was parked in the driveway, but Jake noticed with some relief that there was no sign of Karl's motorbike. As he approached the huge front door, a light came on in a window of one of the turrets. Jake looked up, not sure whether he saw someone hiding behind one of the drapes, so as not to be seen.

Taking a deep breath, he raised the heavy iron knocker and brought it crashing down on the door one, two, three times. He could hear the sound reverberating throughout the house. The place sounded empty and abandoned. If he hadn't seen the light in the upstairs window, he would have thought there was no one at home.

Jake waited for several minutes, while above him the sky grew darker and darker. Finally, just when he was about to give up and go home, he heard a faint pattering from the other side of the door. Someone was coming to see who was foolhardy enough to come calling on Hobb Hill at this time of night.

The door creaked open. Whatever or whoever Jake was expecting, he was not prepared for the old woman who greeted him.

She was tall, over six feet, as thin as the yew branches outside, and clothed in a long black dress. In her right hand she held a large lighted candelabrum. It seemed much too heavy for her bony arm to support.

It was her face that took Jake's breath away: it was the most striking face he had ever seen, as white as the moon which shone in the sky. Her skin was stretched tightly over finely-chiselled cheekbones and an angular chin. Her eyes glittered like two burning coals, and her lips were full and luscious, the colour of freshly spilt blood. Her hair was jet-black, without any hint of grey, and it was pulled tautly back from her face, accentuating its angularity.

This was the aunt of Rebecca and Karl, of that Jake was sure. He recalled the stories which said that the new owner of the house on Hobb Hill was an old silent movie star, a survivor from those far-off days when they had 'faces', and a single flutter of the eyelids on screen could make the entire audience cry. Looking at the old woman's graceful poise and undoubted beauty, he could well believe that.

But there was also a strange air of melancholy and loss about her too, Jake realised. There were other rumours in the area too, that she was the last member of a once-noble family, forced to flee her country in Eastern Europe when it was overrun by revolutionaries. He could believe that as well.

The old woman looked at Jake and licked her lips, as casually as a cat.

'Yes?' Her voice was cracked and ancient, with the faintest trace of an East European accent.

Jake shuffled his feet, suddenly feeling awkward in the presence of this *grande dame*. 'Er ... good evening, ma'am,' he began. 'Is Rebecca at home?'

'Rebecca?' The old woman savoured the sound of the word, as if it were something new to her.

Jake nodded. 'Your niece, Rebecca,' Jake persisted. 'Is she at home?'

The old woman regarded Jake with her piercing black eyes. 'Ah, you are a gentleman caller, are you not? From Castlemare?'

'Excuse me, ma'am?' asked Jake, deciding that there was something extremely weird and spooky about the old woman.

She chuckled. 'Never mind,' she said. 'If you will wait here, I will see if Rebecca is at home.' She slammed the door in Jake's face, and he listened as she walked slowly back down the hallway.

Minutes seemed like hours as Jake waited on the doorstep. He looked up at the lighted window. There was someone there, he was sure, watching him. Every time he looked up, the curtains twitched slightly as someone hid from view.

Night had fallen quickly, and it was now almost pitch black. Apart from the light from the upstairs window, there was no illumination. The street lamps on the road beyond the wall seemed unimaginably distant.

Jake felt as though he had been transported back to a different world, a hundred, two hundred years ago, when frightened, superstitious peasants still bolted their doors in fear of the creatures that haunted the night.

He began to try and steady his nerves, when the heavy oak door was opened once again. The woman was standing there, looking down at Jake with a superior look on her face. He was reminded of Karl's supercilious sneer. *Like aunt, like nephew,* he thought to himself.

'My niece is asleep,' the woman stated in an emotionless monotone. 'She is unable to see anyone tonight.'

Jake frowned and looked down at his Rolex. Nine forty-five. Surely it was too early for Rebecca to go to bed?

'She has had a tiring day,' the woman went on. 'And the night is not for such as she.'

'What do you mean?' Jake asked.

'Good evening, young man,' the woman said and slammed the door in Jake's face.

For a moment, Jake thought of knocking on the door and calling the woman back, but it was obvious that he was going to get no further tonight. He started to shamble down the steps, and make his way back to his waiting car.

As he did so, he looked up at the top-floor window. He was right! There was someone there, looking at him, spying on him. As soon as the person knew that they had been spotted, the light was switched off and the house was plunged into darkness.

Jake made his way back down the path, careful not to trip in the darkness. Above his head he could hear the chirruping of bats in the yew trees, and he shuddered. By the time he reached his car, he found that he was no longer whistling a merry little tune to keep his fears at bay: now he was humming the theme music to *The Addams Family*.

He eased himself into the driver's seat, and was about to turn the ignition key when a motorbike drew up behind the car. Jake looked in the rearview mirror, and saw Karl leap of his bike and come marching up. The blond-haired punk rapped angrily on the window, and Jake wound it down.

Karl shoved his head through the open

window, and glowered angrily at Jake. 'What are you doing here?' he demanded gruffly.

'What's it to you?' Jake replied.

'You've been to see Rebecca, haven't you?' Karl asked, but didn't wait for a reply. 'Stay away from her, you hear? She doesn't want to see you, understand?'

'That's not the impression I got last night,' Jake retorted. 'We seemed to be getting on really well.'

'Stick with your own kind, Yankee boy!' Karl said.

Own kind? 'What d'you mean?' Jake asked, puzzled.

'Our family is one of the oldest and noblest in Europe,' Karl told him. 'We had to leave our country and come here, but Rebecca is still too good for the likes of you, from your jumped-up country across the Atlantic.'

Jake chose to ignore Karl's blatant prejudice. He was much more interested in the fact that Karl and Rebecca came from an old European family. It seemed that the rumours about the old woman in the house on Hobb Hill were right after all.

'Stay away from her, you hear?' Karl repeated. He spat the words out, showing his brilliantly white teeth.

'I think Rebecca should decide for herself, don't you?' Jake said. 'After all, she's old enough, isn't she?'

Karl hesitated for a moment. Then he glanced urgently at the house on the hill, before returning his gaze to Jake. 'Old enough? What do you mean?' he demanded. There was an undisguised note of panic in his voice.

Jake frowned, intrigued by the sudden change in Karl's manner. 'How old is she? Sixteen? Seventeen? She's old enough to make up her own mind now!'

Karl stood back and growled at Jake. *Like a mad dog,* the American thought. *Or a wolf* . . .

'Just stay away from Rebecca, OK?' Karl said, striding over to his motorbike. 'Or you'll be sorry.'

'Is that a threat?'

'If you like,' Karl growled, and revving up his bike he roared up the drive. As he approached the house on Hobb Hill, the bats in the trees *skreeked* out their welcome.

Chapter Five

Jake wandered in a daze through the sets of the film studio. Cameras had been abandoned on the studio floor, to stand like sentinels over the wooden scenery of his father's latest film.

The studio area was open to the sky, and the full moon beamed down on the set, casting macabre shadows and making the 'house on Hell Drive' even more frightening than it was intended to be.

He heard a crunching noise behind him, and turned. A shape was standing there in the distance, watching him. The moon was directly above the figure, and it shone down on her like an overhead light, casting no shadow.

'Rebecca?' he ventured, hoping against hope that this might be the girl of his dreams, the girl he somehow knew he loved above all others.

Rebecca opened her arms wide to welcome him. 'Jake, my love,' she breathed. Her voice was faint and distant, as though it were coming from a long way off. 'Help me. Please, help me . . .'

Jake shook his head. 'I don't understand, Rebecca. How can I help you? What's wrong?'

'They're keeping me prisoner, Jake,' she moaned. Her voice seemed to come not just from the shape Jake presumed to be Rebecca, but from all around him.

'Who? Your aunt and brother?'

Rebecca laughed. 'Yes – only they're not my aunt or my brother,' she complained. 'They're my captors, my gaolers.' She started to sob. 'I want to be free again. Jake, please set me free.'

'Of course,' said Jake, and made to move towards Rebecca.

'No!'

A familiar voice made Jake stop, and he turned to see who was speaking. A klieg light clicked on and the speaker was silhouetted in its icy-blue glare. Jake recognised the old woman from the house on Hobb Hill.

'My niece is asleep. She is unable to see anyone tonight . . .'

They were the same words that she had used on the doorstep, and they were spoken in the same robotic monotone. What the hell was going on? What nightmare had Jake stumbled into?

'Please, Jake,' Rebecca's voice was now a whine, a heart-breaking plea for help. 'Don't listen to her.'

'I only want what is good for you, my child,' the woman claimed.

'She and Karl don't want me to go out into the real world,' said Rebecca. 'They always want me to stay with them, so that they can feed off me like leeches, feed off my youth like . . . like . . .'

Jake stared at Rebecca. What was she trying to say? 'Like what, Rebecca?' he demanded anxiously. 'Feed off your youth like what?'

'Like vampires.'

Rebecca fell to her knees and buried her face in her hands. She sobbed and sobbed, until Jake could bear it no longer. He started to race across the film lot, longing to hold Rebecca in his arms.

At that moment there was a deafening crash, and a motorbike burst through a wooden set, showering Jake in an explosion of splinters. It landed just in front of Jake, cutting him off from Rebecca.

'Please, Jake, come to me now,' Rebecca pleaded.

'My niece is asleep. She is unable to see anyone tonight,' the old woman repeated, seemingly unconcerned at the sudden appearance of Karl on his motorbike.

Jake glared hatefully at Karl, sitting cockily astride the bike. The young Californian clenched his fist, prepared to fight the blond-haired punk to the death if it meant he could save Rebecca from his evil clutches. The veins at his temple throbbed blue with rage. 'Let me get to Rebecca!' he shouted angrily.

Karl shook his head. 'She belongs to us,' he said, and smiled his evil insolent smile. 'She belongs to us both now and forever.'

That twisted smile made something snap in Jake, and he lunged forwards. And then stopped. And then caught his breath. And then drew back in sheer horror.

Karl had drawn back his lips into a horrifying grin, to reveal his brilliantly white teeth. To reveal his two fangs, sparkling terribly in the brilliance of the klieg light. Thick gobbets of warm, sweet, still-fresh blood were dripping from them.

Jake woke with a start, beads of cold sweat pouring from his brow. He shook his head in an attempt to clear his mind. A nightmare, that's what it had been, he realised, a nightmare and nothing more.

He glanced over at his bedside clock radio: 04:47. Jake was normally a heavy sleeper, and he wondered what could have woken him up at this time. He tumbled out of bed and staggered over to the window. He pulled back the curtains and looked out. The first ragged streaks of dawn were pouring over the Heath, heralding a new day.

And in the distance, roaring off down the road, was a motorbike.

Perhaps it hadn't been a dream, after all.

Chapter Six

Crash!

Jake leapt out of his seat, almost knocking over the specimen slides he had lined up on his workbench. Although it was now the summer holidays, Jake had been allowed access to Castlemare's science labs all through the vacation, and he had been working here since early this morning, ever since he had woken up from that terrible nightmare.

He turned round anxiously, trying to identify the source of the noise, and his face broke into a wide grin when he saw Vicky standing behind him. It was she who had frightened him out of his skin, by deliberately dropping a pile of heavy books on to the floor behind him.

'You're alive!' she said sarcastically.

'What do you mean?'

'I've been standing here for the past two minutes, Jake Allan,' she began, folding her arms just like her mother did when she was about to give Vicky one of her all-too-frequent lectures, 'and you didn't even notice me. It was like you were dead to the world!'

Jake laughed, and indicated the microscope on the desk, and the test-tubes, all neatly lined up in their wooden rack. 'I was working on an experiment,' he said. 'I guess I got so wrapped up in it that I didn't hear you come in.'

Vicky shook her head sadly. It was no wonder that Jake didn't have a girlfriend if he spent so much of his time locked up in a science lab. It was the summer vacation, for goodness' sake! He should be out partying, along with her and Sandor! She walked over to the rack of test-tubes and picked one out, holding it up to the light.

'Yuk!' she said as she recognised the reddish-brown sludge within. 'You're still messing around with blood!'

Jake smiled. 'That's right,' he said. 'I told you, I'm trying to come up with a better kind of blood substitute.'

'And how is it that the blood in these test-tubes hasn't clotted?' she asked him. 'After all, whenever I cut myself, after a few seconds the blood dries up.'

'I've added an anti-coagulant,' Jake explained. 'It's similar to the one contained in the saliva of some animals that feed off blood.'

58

Vicky looked curiously at Jake. 'Like bats, you mean . . .'

Jake nodded. 'Vampire bats, yes.'

'You sure know a lot about blood and bats,' Vicky said.

'I'm a scientist, that's all,' Jake said defensively.

'You'd better watch what you say,' Vicky warned him, only half-jokingly. 'Otherwise they'll be spreading the rumour that you're the Castlemare vampire next!'

'What do you mean?' Jake asked urgently.

'There was another killing last night, on the Heath.'

Jake buried his face in his hands. 'Oh, no!'

Vicky knelt down so as to be on a level with Jake. 'Hey, it's OK, it wasn't a human being. It was just a dog this time, an Alsatian.'

'And it had been slaughtered, like Kim . . .'

'That's right,' she said. 'And every drop of blood drained from its body. You can imagine what people are saying . . . Vampires have come to Castlemare!'

'That's stupid,' Jake said, believing in the clear light of day what he would have cause to doubt in the middle of the night. 'Vampires like Count Dracula and the ones in my dad's horror films don't exist. The only true vampires are vampire bats, and they're only found in South America, not in the middle of England!'

'Maybe Sandor brought some over from Argentina?' Vicky suggested fliply, and was surprised at the force of Jake's reaction.

'Don't say that!' he said. 'That's not funny!'

'Sorry,' said Vicky. She looked at Jake's worried face. 'Hey, you really do believe in vampires, don't you?'

Jake refused to answer, and instead looked down at the pile of books which Vicky had brought with her. 'Did you find out anything?' he asked her.

Jake had rung Vicky early that morning to ask a special favour of her as a history student. He had helped her in her chemistry exams last term, so she owed him one.

'I've been working on this all day,' she said, picking up one of the books. 'I hope you realise that I'm going to be late for my date with Sandor tonight?'

Jake arched an eyebrow in interest, and Vicky stuck her tongue out at him. 'And there's no gossip, so you can take that look off your face right now, Jake! We're just going out as friends, that's all!'

'This is a sort of Who's Who of Eastern European families,' she explained, opening the old book. 'It lists all the noble families of any significance, from Bavaria as far as the Ukraine. If Rebecca and Karl's family is as important as Karl says it is, then it should be listed somewhere in this book.'

Vicky stood up and placed the heavy book on Jake's workbench, clearing away some of his test-tubes and slides. Jake offered her his seat, and he peered over her shoulder as she flicked through the pages of the book.

'Vondertoten is a pretty unusual name,' Vicky said, 'so they should be easy to find.' She pointed to an entry. 'There we are. It says here that the Vondertotens were members of the landed gentry in Lithuania.'

'Where's that?' asked Jake, for whom geography was never a particularly strong point.

Vicky shook her head in dismay. 'Don't they teach you Americans anything at school?' she asked good-naturedly.

She took a small atlas from the pile of books on the floor, opened it at a map of Eastern Europe, and pointed to the small country on the north-eastern border of Poland. She chuckled. 'And don't worry, Lithuania's hundreds of miles away from Romania!'

Jake was puzzled. 'Romania? What's in Romania?'

'Transylvania!' Vicky said evilly. 'Vampire country!'

'Don't make fun of me,' Jake said, and Vicky wasn't sure quite how seriously to take her friend.

'Sorry,' she said. 'Do you think Rebecca and Karl could be from Lithuania?'

Jake shrugged. 'Could be. At first I thought they might be German. But one Teutonic accent sounds pretty much the same as another to me.'

Vicky returned to her book. 'Now, this is interesting,' she said. 'It says here that the family died out in that part of Lithuania shortly before the Second World War.'

'Died out?' asked Jake. 'How could that happen?'

'There could be lots of reasons,' Vicky said. 'Maybe the last surviving member of that branch of the family died without leaving an heir. And the Nazis were coming to power then in nearby Germany. Remember the horrible things that they did to people. Whole families were wiped out just because of who they were or because they disagreed with Hitler.'

'What else does the book tell you?' Jake asked.

Vicky slammed the volume shut. 'Nothing,' she said, and reached out for another book. She ran her finger down the index, and then turned to a particular page. 'The family are mentioned here too,' she said, and then her brow furrowed. 'It can't be!'

'What have you found, Vicky?'

'It says here that the family died out in 1941,' she read slowly. 'Their last surviving

62

member was a nineteen-year-old boy. It says that he died of a "a wasting sickness".'

'That was probably tuberculosis,' Jake said. 'What was his name, Vicky? What was the name of the last surviving member of the Vondertoten family?' he asked, even though he already knew the answer.

'Karl,' Vicky said, and an awful wave of dread swept over her. 'His name was Karl.'

Chapter Seven

Hours later, Vicky had left the lab and Jake had continued with his experiments. It was getting dark outside, and finally he decided to pack up for the night. He'd been unable to concentrate on his studies for the past hour anyway.

Why had Karl forbidden him to see Rebecca? Who was the mysterious old woman who lived in the old house on Hobb Hill? And was Karl really a vampire, or was Jake letting his imagination run away with him? After all, he had no real evidence, just a deep nagging feeling deep down inside. That, and the brutal way in which Kim had been murdered. And the fact that they had never yet seen Karl in the daytime.

Jake, my man, a guy stops you from seeing his sister, and you start imagining all sorts of things about him! he tried to reason with himself, as he started to lock his instruments away in the storeroom cupboard.

He stacked the test-tubes and his attempts

to fabricate a better blood-plasma substitute away too. He wasn't having much success with his experiments, and if he didn't make a breakthrough tomorrow, then he'd probably have to give up on them.

As he passed the window, he thought he saw something move out of the corner of his eye. He pressed his face to the pane of glass: nothing. Just the same old yew trees that had grown in the grounds of Castlemare for hundreds of years, silhouetted against the light of the waning moon. No monsters from his dad's horror pics, no demon-beasts from hell, and definitely no vampires! It was probably only an owl in one of the trees.

And yet . . . And yet, Jake remembered the last surviving member of the Vondertoten family, the young guy who had died of TB in Lithuania just as the Second World War was getting under way. *Karl Vondertoten*, the same name as Rebecca's brother. Were he and the punk biker they had met one and the same person?

Jake, tomorrow morning you are going to ring your old man up and persuade him to give you a job script-writing his next horror movie, Jake chuckled to himself. *Because with the imagination you've got, you could really go places in that business!*

Vampires didn't exist in the twentieth century, Jake told himself, and he knew that

Vicky was right when she told him that the two Karls were just a coincidence. Karl, after all, was a common name.

He was about to lock the door to the lab, when he heard a shuffling sound at the far end of the corridor. He had been right! Someone was there, spying on him. He peered down the corridor, but it was in darkness, and he couldn't see. He raised his hand and glided it along the wall, searching for the light switch.

'Who's there?' he called out. 'I know you're there. Come and show yourself.'

There was no reply, but Jake could hear a laboured heavy breathing coming from the shadows. With his whole body tensed, ready for whatever might happen, he flicked the light switch and the corridor was suddenly bathed in a harsh, bright light.

'Rebecca?'

She was standing at the other end of the corridor, wearing the same long cloak and red dress as before. She shielded her eyes from the brilliance of the electric light.

'Jake!' Rebecca gasped. 'Thank goodness it's you!' She lowered her hands, now that her eyes had grown accustomed to the light, and ran towards Jake. There were tears streaming down her face as she flung her arms around him.

'Rebecca! What's wrong?' he asked, genuinely concerned at her obvious distress.

'I prayed I would find you here,' she said. 'They don't know that I've left the house.'

'They? You mean, Karl and your aunt?'

'That's right,' she sobbed, burying her head in Jake's shoulder and wrapping her arms around his neck. 'You don't know what it's like, being locked up in that house all day and all night, and only being allowed out when they say so.'

'Locked up?' This sounded serious to Jake, illegal even. 'Look, if they're holding you against your will, you should go to the police.'

Rebecca pulled herself away from him and shook her head sadly. 'They wouldn't believe me,' she said. 'My aunt is a very rich woman and is very powerful. She would tell them that what she was doing was for my own good.'

'Let me take you with me,' Jake said. 'You'll be safe at my flat.'

Rebecca shook her head again. 'Not now,' she said, 'not tonight. They'll soon see I'm missing. But tomorrow night they're both going to be out. Perhaps then. You will come for me then, won't you? You won't let yourself be turned away, like you were last time?'

'Last time?' Jake didn't know what she was talking about.

'Last night,' Rebecca said. 'I was watching you from the upstairs window. My aunt told you I was asleep, but I wasn't.'

'Rebecca, you should have called out to me!' Jake said. The young girl hung her head.

'And risked Karl's anger?' she said mournfully. 'He was upstairs in the room with me. You don't know how cruel he can be to me. If I'd called out, he would have hit me.'

Jake put a finger underneath Rebecca's chin, and raised her head gently so that she was looking straight into his eyes. 'Rebecca, why are they keeping you locked away like this?' he demanded softly.

Rebecca shrugged. 'Perhaps they don't realise that I'm now a grown woman, that I want to live like other people my own age,' she said, looking at Jake fondly. 'That I want to live with people like you . . .'

'Rebecca . . .' Jake smiled down at her and wiped her eyes. 'Your face is all tear-stained,' he said. 'You want a mirror so you can tidy yourself up?'

Rebecca tensed in his arms. 'N-no,' she said. She cocked her head, in the way Jake had seen cats do when they heard something a long way off, something which no human ears could hear. 'There's no time for that now,' she gasped. 'I must go before Karl discovers I'm missing.'

'Tomorrow night,' Jake began.

'Be at the house tomorrow at dusk,' Rebecca said. 'Go round the back, to the

69

tradesmen's entrance. And don't tell anyone that you're going to be there – it must be our secret!'

She reached up and kissed him, a long deep kiss on the lips. Then she broke away abruptly. 'I have to go now,' she said, and turned and ran back down the corridor, her cape fluttering behind her.

'Rebecca, wait!' Jake cried, and ran after her, out through the great double doors which led into the Castlemare car park. He stopped: Rebecca was nowhere to be seen. There were only the yew tees, their branches swaying gently in the wind, mocking him.

'There you are,' he heard someone say. 'All work and no play makes Jake the dullest person on the face of this planet, *sabe, amigo*?'

'Sandor, what are you doing here?' Jake asked.

'Come to drag you away from your test-tubes and Bunsen burners, and take you to a real party!' Sandor said happily. 'Vicky told me how down in the dumps you were, so you are going out with us tonight!'

'Did you see her?' Jake asked.

'See who?'

'Rebecca. She was here just a few seconds ago.'

Sandor shook his head. 'There has been no one here but me.' He looked up at the moon, and the tiny creatures flying across its face. 'And the bats, of course.'

'You must have seen her,' Jake insisted.

'No,' Sandor said. 'You have been working too hard, *amigo*. Perhaps you imagined it. You need a break. So tonight Vicky and I are taking you to the best party in town!'

'Don't be stupid, Sandor,' Jake said. 'I don't want to play gooseberry with you and Vicky.'

'Ah, but you will not be,' Sandor told him. 'Sara is coming along too. And if you both get along, then maybe we can all go out tomorrow night as well!'

Jake shook his head, as he walked with Sandor to his car. 'Not tomorrow,' he told his best friend firmly. 'Tomorrow I'm doing something very important indeed.'

As they drove out of the car park, neither of them noticed Karl's motorbike as it came out of its hiding place behind a large clump of bushes and slowly turned down the drive. Karl drove up to the science labs, shut down the engine and leapt off the motorbike.

He looked around, making sure that he was alone. There was no sign of life, apart from a tiny light winking in a small shed at the far end of the school grounds. That came from Mr Bream's office, he guessed, and he knew that the school caretaker would be making his rounds in – Karl looked at his watch – about fifteen minutes. Time, then, was of the essence.

A high-pierced squeaking made him jump. He turned around, fists clenched and at the ready. And then he laughed, as he saw a bat flutter past. 'You wouldn't hurt me, would you, my pretty?' he whispered, and then turned back to the task in hand.

He sneaked along the side of the science building, pressing his body close to the wall and keeping as much as possible out of the light of the moon, which threw his shadow in massive relief on the gravelled path. Finally he reached the window which looked into the science lab, where Jake had been working earlier.

Karl glanced up. Above the window there was an alarm box. With an almost supernatural agility, Karl leapt on to the ground-floor window ledge and reached up to the alarm. He took a knife out of his pocket and began to saw away at the wire which connected the alarm to the rest of the main alarm system.

Satisfied that the alarm was now disabled, Karl leapt off the window-sill, making not a sound as his boots hit the ground. He took his jacket off and wrapped it around his fist, before smashing the glass of the window pane and leaping into the lab.

Karl knew exactly where he was headed:

after all, he had been watching Jake for most of the afternoon. It had been a close call when Jake thought he was being spied upon, but Karl had managed to stay out of sight behind one of the yew trees.

He strode up to the cupboard in which Jake had locked his equipment, and took the padlock in his hands. With one superhuman wrench, he ripped the lock away and opened the cupboard. As he rummaged around, a cardboard folder fell to the floor. He picked it up and casually cast his eyes over the paper which had fallen out. They were notes which Jake had made some time ago, and as Karl read them, he licked his lips.

'Type AB,' he said. 'Of course, what could be more perfect.'

He stood there for a moment, thinking, and then dropped the folder back onto the floor. It had told him everything he wanted to know and he no longer had any need of it.

He took out the test-tubes of blood and uncorked them, one by one. He raised each of them to the moonlight streaming in through the broken window, considering their colour. Then he sniffed at them, savouring the delicate bouquet of Jake's blood-samples. In the moonlight Karl Vondertoten looked just like a wine connoisseur, examining a fine claret or Burgundy before drinking it.

Chapter Eight

The Inferno was one of the trendiest and most happening discos in town, the sort where you were only allowed in if you knew the doorman and where a round of drinks at the bar cost about the same as most people would spend on a slap-up meal. Needless to say, it was incredibly popular with all the students from nearby Castlemare High.

Jake, Sara, Sandor and Vicky were sitting at a table on one of the gantries suspended over the main dance floor, watching the hot and heavy action down below.

The DJ was playing an extremely eclectic range of tracks. In the past hour Jake had heard samples of '70s disco, '80s punk, '90s heavy metal and something which sounded suspiciously like a rocking version of Beethoven's Ninth. The ravers on the dance floor reflected that variety.

There were dancers wearing classy Montana suits and revealing Versace dresses; ravers wearing baseball caps, cut-off shorts and very little else; rockers and bikers, clad head to foot in leather and chains; and people like Jake, dressed in simple T-shirts and 501s. All of them, however, had one thing in common – they were all devastatingly good-looking. That, after all, was another of the entry requirements for the Inferno.

Sara jogged Jake's arm. 'C'mon, Jake, let's dance,' she said. 'You've been sitting watching other people move for long enough now. It's almost as if you were searching the crowd for someone!'

Jake turned and looked at Sara. 'Later, OK?' he told the pretty long-haired girl. 'I'm not in the mood right now.'

Sandor, who was sitting back in his chair with his arm casually draped over Vicky's shoulder, laughed. 'Perhaps Jake is looking for one particular person, *si*?'

Jake glared angrily at him. 'Leave it out, Sandor,' he said.

Vicky agreed with Jake. 'Stop teasing him, Sandor,' she said. 'You never know, Rebecca might be here.'

Jake shook his head. 'She won't be here.'

'Rebecca?' asked Sara. 'Who's Rebecca?' Sandor reminded her of the girl she had seen briefly at the bar the other night. Sara nodded, and then grinned. 'The one with her tongue halfway down Jake's throat – I remember. The vamp in the black cape.'

'What did you call her?' Jake's tone was urgent, worried.

Sara shrugged: she couldn't see what the problem was. 'The vamp in the black cape . . .'

'Vamp, Jake, not vampire,' Vicky said, smiling at her friends. 'Jake's been obsessed with vampires lately, ever since Kim's murder.'

'And that dog found out on the Heath too,' Jake said. 'Drained of all its blood.'

Sandor and Vicky laughed, ribbing Jake good-naturedly. Sara, however, was deadly serious. 'They couldn't have been vampires,' she said with certainty. 'Real vampires don't behave like that.'

Sandor exchanged an amused look with Vicky, which Sara caught.

'When I say real vampires, I mean the way they're depicted in the old legends,' she said. Jake began to listen carefully. Sara, with her other-worldly aura, and her interest in the supernatural, could be counted something of an expert on these matters. 'They're careful killers. They wouldn't savage a body like Jake says Kim had been.'

Jake shuddered: the image of Kim, her body ripped open and eviscerated, was still fresh in his memory. When he discovered her on his early-morning run, he had wanted to throw up. Someone else already had, he re-membered, recalling the stomach-churning pool of bile by Kim's carcass.

'Now you don't seriously believe in vam-pires, do you?' Vicky asked Sara, and glanced over at Jake. He was once again looking down at the dance floor.

'There are vampire legends in most countries of the world,' Sara said. 'Of blood-sucking creatures who only go out at night. Of monsters who can change into bats or wolves, and who never cast a shadow or show a reflection.'

'And who can only be killed by a wooden stake through the heart,' Sandor scoffed. 'I've seen my fair share of Dracula movies too, you know!'

'Then you'll also know that they can't stand the sight of a crucifix,' Sara said. 'And that they can't cross over running water.'

'And I also know that you'll never find vampires in France,' Sandor sneered.

'And why's that?' Sara asked.

'Too much garlic in the cooking,' he said.

Vicky smiled. 'Something tells me that Sandor isn't taking you too seriously, Sara,' she said.

Sara glowered at the cocky Argentinian. 'Well, then he should,' she said. 'If he spent more time examining the mysteries of this world, and less using his smooth Latin

American charms on anything with a pulse and a skirt . . .'

'Hey, you are out of order there,' Sandor said.

'Am I?' Sara said.

Vicky tried to come between the two of them. 'Hey, now come on,' she said, 'We've come here to have fun, not start another English-Argentinian war!'

'Wait a moment, Vicky,' Sandor said and leant forward angrily at Sara. 'Do I detect a little bit of envy here?' he asked cruelly. 'I seem to recall last year that you tried to ask me out, Sara, and I turned you down flat. So it looks as though I won't just go out with anything with a pulse and a skirt. Maybe I do have some standards, after all.'

Things were starting to become nasty, and Jake turned away from the dance floor to try and ease the tension. 'Hey, now lighten up, you guys,' he said.

Sara ignored Jake and continued to stare at Sandor. 'You just use people all the time, Sandor,' she said. 'That's why you've never had a steady girlfriend, because you can't handle the give and take in a relationship. You go out with a girl for a couple of nights and then you dump her because you've taken all you can from her. You're . . . you're like a vampire!'

Sandor stood up. 'I don't have to listen to

this,' he said, and stormed off the gantry and down the spiral staircase to the dance floor.

When he had gone, Vicky looked reprovingly at Sara. 'You shouldn't have said that, you know,' she said, and then added: 'Even if it was true.'

'Sandor's a nice guy really,' Jake said. 'You just don't know him as well as Vicky and I do.'

'All I know is what I see,' Sara said flatly.

'Then you shouldn't judge by appearances,' Vicky urged her gently. 'Why don't you go down and apologise?'

'He's been down there half a minute already,' said Sara. 'He's probably already chatting up some new girl. I wouldn't want to cramp his style!' Even Vicky smiled at this.

Sara stood up. 'I'm going out for a breath of fresh air,' she said. 'You coming?'

Both shook their head, and Sara left them.

'So now it's just you and me,' Vicky said to Jake. 'You've had something on your mind all evening, Jake. You've been staring down at that dance floor like you were searching for someone. What's the matter?'

Jake laughed. 'You probably think I'm mad,' he said. 'And you're bound to tell me that I'm obsessed. But earlier this evening, down there on the dance floor, I could have sworn I saw Karl.'

'Karl Vondertoten? Are you sure?'

Jake shrugged. 'Maybe. It was only for a second, but I recognised the back of his head with that peroxide hair, and his leather jacket.'

Vicky pointed to the crowds on the dance floor. 'Jake, half the guys down there are wearing leather jackets, with peroxide hair!' she said. 'And what if Karl is here tonight? It's a free country, isn't it? Besides, I would have thought that if you were looking out for anyone, it would be Rebecca.'

Jake shook his head sadly, thinking of Rebecca locked up in that tiny room in the house on Hobb Hill.

'No,' he said. 'I know that Rebecca won't be here . . . not tonight.'

Sara slammed the door behind her and breathed deeply of the fresh air, in the tiny alleyway outside the Inferno. Beyond the door, she could still hear the throb of the music, feel the heat from the hundreds of dancers.

Damn Sandor! she said to herself. They were so different from each other, like chalk and cheese. They would never get on together, no matter how hard Sara tried. But then she was always putting her foot in it, just like tonight. Sandor had been right when he said that she was jealous of all the other girls he had been out with, and annoyed that he had turned her down. *But why did he have to be so blasted smug about it?*

She shivered. It had suddenly grown very cold, and she thought of going back inside. A cloud obscured the moon, and she was suddenly aware of someone standing next to her.

'Do you have a cigarette?' the person asked.

Sara shook her head. 'Sorry,' she said, and when she recognised the person, added: 'And neither should you.'

'Ah well, I do lots of things that I shouldn't, don't I?'

Sara frowned. 'What do you mean?'

'It doesn't matter,' came the reply. 'What does matter, however, is your telling all our little secrets.'

'Little secrets? I don't understand.'

'People don't believe in us these days. That's why we are never caught, because people don't know how to. And then you go and give away all our secrets – wooden stakes, running water, no reflection . . .'

Sara's breath caught in her throat. She backed away, towards the door.

But it was too late. She felt a hand around her throat, a hand so supernaturally strong that she couldn't break free. The hand tightened its grip, squeezing all the air out of her body.

The moon came out from its cloud cover, and Sara saw the moonbeams glint on the sharpened fangs. She smelt the creature's fetid breath, as it pressed its mouth to her throat, experienced a pain she had never imagined in her wildest nightmares, as the mighty fangs ripped at her white, soft flesh.

Ten minutes later, Kirsty and Marc, two students from Castlemare, opened the door to the alleyway where they were planning to have a crafty snog. When they saw Sara's gutted and bloody body, the head lolling at an unnatural angle and almost wrenched off its shoulders, they suddenly forgot all about romance.

Chapter Nine

Sandor looked up and smiled weakly when he recognised his two visitors. He had been crying, and there were dark rings under his eyes. His normally immaculately combed and slicked-back hair was dishevelled, and he was still wearing the shirt and jeans he had been in last night at the Inferno disco.

'Hi Jake, Vicky,' he said. His voice was cracked and dry: he had, after all, been talking to the police for over ten hours now, ever since they had arrested him at six o'clock that morning.

Jake looked uncertainly at the police sergeant who was standing at the far end of the tiny little room. The policeman nodded, indicating that they could sit on the two wooden chairs by the small table which separated them from Sandor.

'Are you all right?' Vicky asked. 'Are they treating you OK?'

Sandor nodded. 'They're going to charge me with Sara's murder, you know.'

'That's crazy!' Jake cried out, and then lowered his voice at a warning glance from the policeman on duty. 'That's stupid. Why would you want to kill Sara?'

'Someone saw me arguing with her last night,' Sandor replied.

'But you were down on the dance floor!' Vicky protested.

'Did you see me?' Sandor asked. Vicky shook her head: there had been so many people there. In fact, for the rest of the night neither of them had set eyes on the young Argentinian, and in the end Jake had had to drive Vicky home in his car, presuming that Sandor and Sara had each made their separate ways home.

'We know you couldn't have killed Sara,' Jake reassured his best friend. 'Why didn't you tell them where you were?'

'I tried to,' Sandor said, burying his face in his hands. 'But I couldn't prove it. I met this real sexy girl on the dance floor, you see . . .'

Vicky looked disapprovingly at her friend. 'And you spent most of the night with her?' she asked.

Sandor nodded. 'We stayed till five o'clock, when the club was beginning to empty out.'

Jake couldn't see what the problem was. 'So you must have been together when Sara was killed,' he said. 'That girl's your alibi. All you need is to get her to come forward and verify your story to the police.'

Sandor looked up, almost sheepishly, at Jake. 'Ah, well, that's the problem,' he said. 'You see, I forgot to ask her what her name was . . .'

It was now Jake's turn to bury his face in his hands. 'Oh, man, I knew nothing good was going to come from your philandering one day,' he moaned. 'What do you mean, you never asked her name?'

'Exactly what I said!' Sandor snapped back 'We were having a great time dancing, and then we got into a pretty serious clinch in the chill-out room. It never occurred to me to ask what her name was.'

Vicky sighed. *What is it about men?* she asked herself. At times it seemed that they thought about only one thing – and it certainly wasn't names!

'So, what's going to happen now?' she asked, deciding that one of them ought to show some common sense.

'I'm going to be officially charged with Sara's murder,' Jake said. 'And then I guess I'll be locked up until my trial.'

Jake slammed his fist angrily into the palm of his other hand. 'This is crazy, they can't just keep you locked up like a common criminal. I thought you were supposed to be innocent until proven guilty in this country?'

He thought back to all those series he'd watched back home in the States. What happened in similar cases in *Columbo* or

Murder, She Wrote? 'What about bail?' he asked excitedly. 'You've never been in trouble with the police before – or have you?'

'No,' Sandor replied firmly.

'Then surely they can let you out on bail?' Jake reasoned. Sandor nodded.

'Sure,' he said, 'Detective Sergeant Ashby took great delight in telling me what he's going to recommend my bail to be.'

'That's great,' Vicky said. 'Let's just raise the money, and get you out of here!'

Sandor gave an ironic smile. 'And would you mind telling me where we're going to get our hands on two hundred thousand pounds?'

Jake whistled. 'Two hundred grand! That's way out of order, man,' he said.

'You know how much Ashby hates the rich kids of Castlemare,' Sandor said. 'I guess that this is his way of getting his own back.'

'But can't your parents help you?' Jake asked.

Sandor shook his head. 'They're out of the country,' he replied, 'halfway up the Amazon, miles from the nearest telephone. I won't be able to contact them for at least a week.'

Vicky looked at Jake. 'What about your dad?' she asked. 'Could he raise the money?'

'He's a producer of schlock horror movies,' Jake said. 'There's no way he could lay his hands on that sort of cash.'

'So it looks as though I'm going to stay here until my trial,' Sandor said despondently. 'Unless someone raises my bail – or we find out who really did kill Sara.'

The door opened and Detective Sergeant Ashby entered. He smirked when he saw the three of them huddled around the table. That's how he liked to see the rich kids of Castlemare – brought down a peg or two. That would show them that they weren't quite as special as they liked to think they were!

'Visiting hour's over,' he chuckled. 'Time for you two to get back to your penthouse flats, while my laddo here gets ready to spend his first night in the cells!'

Vicky stared Ashby in the eyes. 'We can't leave him here,' she said firmly. 'We must see him later.'

Ashby shook his head. 'Rules are rules,' he said. 'Only one visit a day.'

'I am sure Miss Greystone would be very grateful if we could see our friend later tonight,' Vicky said. She knew the high regard in which Detective Sergeant Ashby held the Principal of Castlemare High. She also knew of the large sums Miss Greystone put into the Police Benevolent Fund.

Ashby harrumphed. 'Well, I suppose that might be possible,' he said.

'Thank you,' Vicky said frostily.

Ashby started to lead Jake and Vicky out of the room, and shook his head. 'I don't know what it is about you rich kids,' he said. 'You murder someone . . .'

'Sandor has not murdered anyone!' Jake exploded. 'And he has not been declared guilty!'

'You get yourselves accused of murder, and everyone's flocking to see you,' he continued. 'If I'd known, I'd've started selling tickets!'

'What do you mean, everyone's coming to see me?' Sandor asked.

'You had another visitor about half an hour ago,' Ashby said.

For a moment Sandor hoped it might have been the girl with whom he had spent the night dancing, and who could provide him with his alibi.

'Who was she?' he asked.

'It was a he, not a she,' Ashby said. 'Sorry to disappoint you!'

'Then why didn't you let him in to see Sandor?' Vicky demanded.

'Rules are rules, young lady,' Ashby repeated. 'You two were with your friend at the time, and he couldn't have two sets of guests. We're not running a holiday camp here, you know!'

'Who was it?' Sandor demanded angrily.

'I didn't catch his name,' the policeman

said. 'But he said that he'd heard on the grapevine that you'd been arrested for murder. He also wanted to know what your bail was. And then he drove away. A surly, obnoxious character, if you ask me.'

'*Drove away*?' asked Jake.

Ashby nodded. 'That's right . . . on his motorbike.'

Karl!

Chapter Ten

Jake parked his car at the bottom of Hobb
Hill and covered the rest of the distance on
foot. Rebecca had assured him that her aunt
and Karl would both be out for the night, but
he didn't want to take any chances.

It was almost ten o'clock and darkness had
fallen over Hobb Hill. In the yew trees the
bats were already chirping, readying themselves for their night-time hunt. Not for the
first time, Jake thought it strange that there
should be so many bats in this area of North
London. He would have expected them in the
countryside, or in Sandor's homeland of
Latin America, but not here. Sara would
have made something sinister of that, he
knew.

But Sara is dead! he reminded himself.
Slaughtered by Karl Vondertoten, if his sus-
picions were correct, *ripped apart by the very
person who was keeping Rebecca a prisoner
in the old house on Hobb Hill!*

He finally reached Rebecca's house. Once

again, the old Gothic folly was in darkness, apart from a light shining from one of the turrets, from Rebecca's bedroom window.

He creaked open the rusty gate and started walking up the path. Karl's motorbike wasn't parked in the drive, and neither was the old limousine he had seen the other night and which he presumed belonged to Rebecca's aunt. It seemed his girlfriend was right: tonight she was going to be alone in the house.

His girlfriend! The words sounded unfamiliar, yet at the same time wonderful. Jake had only known Rebecca for a few days, he realised, but already she had made herself so much a part of his life. He would have done anything for her: he was caught in her spell.

Jake remembered what Rebecca had told him: *'Be at the house tomorrow at dusk. Go round the back, to the tradesmen's entrance. And don't tell anyone that you're going to be there – it must be our secret!*

He made his way through the undergrowth – it seemed naïve to expect Rebecca's aunt ever to mow her lawn – and went round the back of the house. As he approached the door which, he supposed, led to what used to be the servants' quarters, a light was flicked on in the downstairs window.

Jake froze. Had Karl or Rebecca's aunt unexpectedly returned to the house? To his relief he heard Rebecca's voice from the other side of the door: 'Jake, is that you?'

'Rebecca, I'm here,' he whispered, and the door opened. Rebecca was standing there, wearing her black cape. Her eyes darted this way and that, as if she was making sure that they were truly alone.

She ran towards Jake and flung herself into his arms. 'I'm so glad that you've come for me,' she said. 'You don't know how terrified I've been!'

Jake ran his hands up and down the small of Rebecca's back. Even though it was the height of summer, the poor girl seemed frozen solid. Jake realised that she was obviously very frightened indeed.

'Hey, it's OK,' he reassured her, and nuzzled her ear. 'I'm here now, you've nothing to worry about.'

Rebecca looked up at Jake, with her narrow and unblinking eyes. 'You promise me that, Jake?' she begged. 'You'll be with me forever?'

'Of course I will,' Jake replied, and felt Rebecca tense in his arms. 'What's wrong?'

'We must get away from here now!' Rebecca said.

'It's OK,' Jake said. 'You told me yourself that Karl and your aunt are out for the night.'

'Did I?' For a half-instant Rebecca seemed

confused. Then she recovered her senses. 'Of course I did,' she said. 'But they will be back soon. We must go somewhere they cannot find us – ever again.'

'Come back to my flat,' Jake urged her. 'My parents are away.'

'No,' Rebecca said firmly. 'Karl has seen how much . . ., how much . . .' She looked coyly at Jake. 'We are in love with each other, aren't we, Jake?'

Jake smiled. 'I've only known you for days, but you've bewitched me, Rebecca,' he admitted. 'Yes, I do love you.'

'Good!' Rebecca said, almost triumphantly, and then continued: 'Karl has seen how much we are in love with each other, and your flat will be the first place he will look. Is there anywhere else we can go? Somewhere Karl would never think of looking? Somewhere private?'

'There's the film studios!' Jake said.

'The film studios?'

'On the outskirts of town,' Jake said. 'It would only take us about an hour to get there in the car. My dad's filming his movie there!'

'But surely there will be security there night and day?' asked Rebecca.

'No problem,' Jake said, pulling a plastic pass from the back pocket of his 501s. 'I'm the producer's son, and I have Access All Areas!'

'And in this film studio Karl will not be able to find us?'

Jake shook his head. 'The only people who might guess I could be there would be Sandor and Vicky,' he said.

'Then that is good,' Rebecca said, and allowed Jake to lead her to his car. 'I want to be with you forever, Jake, just you and me, together alone.'

'That's what I want too, Rebecca,' Jake said, and kissed her on the lips. 'I do love you, Rebecca.'

'And I love you too, Jake,' she said, and then paused, before asking: 'You said your father was a film producer. What sort of movies does he make?'

Jake smiled. 'Don't you remember? On the last night of term when we first met, you told me that they were your favourite type of movies. He makes horror films!'

Rebecca smiled. 'Of course,' she said. 'How silly of me to forget ... Horror movies ... How very appropriate.'

Vicky held Sandor's hands in hers and kissed them, as a good friend would. 'I'm sorry,' she said.

'The cells are horrible, Vicky,' Sandor admitted. 'And everyone here thinks that I killed Sara.'

'Well, I know you didn't,' she said for what

97

seemed like the hundredth time today. She looked up at the wall clock in the tiny visiting room: it was half past ten, and outside the police station it was pitch black. 'It was good of Ashby to let me see you again today.'

'Yes, that surprised me,' Sandor said. 'How did you manage it?'

Vicky grinned. 'It seemed that my little threat to have Miss Greystone cut off the money to the Benevolent Fund worked!'

'Where's Jake?' Sandor asked.

Vicky shrugged. 'I don't know,' she said. 'I rang his flat before I came here and all I got was his answerphone.'

'He's probably seeing Rebecca,' Sandor said.

Suddenly the door to the visiting room opened, and Detective Sergeant Ashby poked his head around the door. He regarded Sandor through narrow, distrusting eyes.

'You're in luck, my laddo,' he said, through clenched teeth. 'You can go!'

Sandor stood up, scarcely believing what Ashby was telling him. 'What? You mean, you think I'm innocent? You believe I didn't kill Sara after all?'

Ashby sneered. 'Nothing so spectacular, I'm afraid,' he said. 'You're still to go to trial. But some fool has just coughed up your bail!'

Sandor and Vicky exchanged puzzled and

amazed looks. 'Someone's paid my bail?' Sandor asked disbelievingly. 'Someone's paid two hundred thousand pounds?'

'The woman's a damn fool if you ask me,' Ashby said, and then flushed red with embarrassment, as he realised that the woman he was talking about could hear him. He turned to her. She was still obscured by the half-open door, and Sandor and Vicky could not see who she was.

'No offence meant, ma'am,' he flustered.

'And no offence taken, Ashby,' Sandor and Vicky heard a husky feminine voice say. 'Now, please leave me alone with Sandor.'

'Of course, ma'am,' said Ashby and left the room. The door opened to reveal a tall woman in a black dress standing in the doorway. She looked closely at both Sandor and Vicky, as though she were examining specimens in a zoo, and then walked into the room.

'You are Sandor?' she asked of the young Argentinian.

Sandor nodded. 'Th-that's right,' he stammered. 'Did you pay my bail?'

The woman nodded. Vicky guessed that she must be at least sixty. 'That is correct,' she said. 'All two hundred thousand pounds of it.'

'But why?' Sandor asked. 'We've never met before.'

'That is true,' the woman said. 'But I also know that you did not kill the young child called Sara last night.'

'But how?'

'Because I know who did,' she stated, as calmly and as nonchalantly as if she were reporting on the state of the weather. 'Karl has admitted everything to me.'

Karl! Karl Vondertoten! Jake had been right after all!

'You're Rebecca and Karl's aunt!' Vicky suddenly realised. 'You're the old lady who lives in the house on Hobb Hill!'

'I am indeed the woman who lives on the house on Hobb Hill,' the old lady admitted, and then smirked. 'Although I do take issue with the description "old"! After all, I am only sixty-five.'

'Sorry,' Vicky said, realising, unlike Sandor, just how touchy women were about their age.

'And Karl is not my nephew,' the old woman continued. 'He is my dearly beloved grandson. And Rebecca . . .'

'Yes?' Sandor urged her on. What relation was the beautiful young Rebecca to this sexagenarian?

'Rebecca is my older sister . . .'

Chapter Eleven

The parchment-coloured moon shone down on the open-air film lot, as Jake led Rebecca through to the *House on Hell Drive* set. It had been relatively easy to get past the dozing security guard, who upon seeing the producer's son had simply assumed that he was taking his new girlfriend for a midnight tryst and had promptly dozed off again. Now Rebecca was wandering among the abandoned cameras and lighting equipment, as though in a dream.

'You're sure you're OK?' Jake asked. 'You were so quiet in the car coming here.'

'I am fine now,' Rebecca said, and continued to examine the set of the movie. They were in what appeared to be the keep of a ruined castle, surrounded by three 'stone' walls; there was no fourth wall so that the camera could film within the set.

'It is all so lifelike,' Rebecca said, running her hand along the 'stonework' of the set's walls.

'All wood and cardboard,' Jake said. 'The stone walls of this castle would never keep any marauding hordes out!'

'It reminds me of the castles back home,' Rebecca said, 'in Lithuania.'

So Vicky had been right! Rebecca's family did come from that Eastern European country! Jake moved over to Rebecca and put his arms around her waist. 'Rebecca, I know so little about you,' he began, but she turned to face him and put a silencing finger to his lips.

'You know that you love me,' she said, 'and that I love you. Surely that is enough.'

Jake smiled. 'I thought that the Vondertotens of Lithuania had all died out,' he said, remembering the old books that Vicky had shown him.

For a moment Rebecca frowned, but then she smiled and tapped Jake playfully on the nose. 'Have you been spying on me?' she asked.

'No,' Jake said. 'But I remember reading in a book that the last family member died in the early 1940s. His name was Karl.'

'Yes, I remember, "the wasting sickness",' Rebecca said. 'My brother Karl was named after him. But the book was wrong: the family did not quite die out. After all, I am alive, aren't I?'

'I love you so much, Rebecca,' Jake said.

'And I want to help you. Why are your aunt and Karl holding you prisoner in the house on Hobb Hill?'

Rebecca shivered, and Jake held her closer in his arms. She felt so cold.

'They want me to be like them,' Rebecca said, wrapping her arms around Jake and bringing his face down to hers.

She kissed him on the lips, a long, deep kiss which set Jake's pulse racing. She ran her fingers through his closely-cropped hair, and then along his neck, feeling the pulse of his jugular vein. She pulled back and smiled.

'You have very large veins,' she said.

Jake laughed: he had received compliments before from girls, but none like this! 'Full of the rarest blood group in the world!' he bragged.

'Don't be silly,' Rebecca said, and added meaningfully: 'There are blood sub-groups rarer than AB . . .'

Jake frowned. 'How did you know my blood group?' he asked. 'I didn't tell you.'

'I smelt it,' Rebecca said, almost flippantly. 'Now, kiss me again.'

Jake kissed Rebecca on the lips. In his arms the girl was becoming more and more excited and he felt her respond with an ardour equal to his own, felt her lips on his own lips, felt them on his cheeks, on his neck . . .

Click!

Suddenly the whole set was bathed in a painfully white brilliance. Someone had switched on all the klieg lights, surrounding Jake and Rebecca with a circle of light. Jake pulled away from Rebecca and shaded his eyes to see who had turned on the lights. Two figures appeared from out of the brilliance and walked slowly towards them.

'Sandor! Vicky!' Jake cried. 'What are you doing here? How did you get past security?'

'Our friend bribed the guard,' Sandor said, and nodded towards the old lady who was following them into the circle of light.

Jake recognised the figure of Rebecca's aunt. Rebecca hissed.

'Your friend? I don't understand,' Jake said. 'She's the one who's been holding Rebecca prisoner in the house on Hobb Hill!'

Vicky shook her head and held her hand out to Jake. 'Come to us, Jake,' she urged. 'You're in danger.'

Jake looked at Rebecca, who seemed as puzzled as he was. Then he turned back to his friends. 'Danger? What sort of danger?'

'Vampires,' said Sandor.

Rebecca hissed again. 'Don't listen to them, Jake!' she said.

The old lady walked forwards, and looked sadly at Rebecca and Jake. 'For over forty years I have looked after my older sister, Rebecca, ever since the day she died.'

'Rebecca, what is she talking about?' Jake asked, confused. 'How can she be your sister – she's over sixty years old!'

'She's mad, that's what she is!' Rebecca said. 'She's mad, mad, mad!'

'Come away from her, Jake!' Sandor cried. 'Look at Rebecca's shadow.'

Jake looked down at the shadows on the floor caused by the light from the kliegs. There was his shadow, and next to it . . . Next to it was nothing!

Rebecca was casting no shadow!

'Rebecca has no shadow, because she's a vampire,' Vicky said sadly. 'Her aunt – her younger sister – has told us everything.'

Rebecca grabbed Jake's hand, holding it in a clasp of steel. 'Don't listen to them, Jake!' she said. 'They've all been poisoned against me!'

'It wasn't Karl who killed Sara and Kim,' Sandor said. 'It was Rebecca!'

'She needed blood to keep her alive,' the old woman said. 'My grandson, Karl, and I would slaughter animals for her, like that Alsatian that was found on the Heath. But she wanted more. The times she escaped from Hobb Hill, she went out in search of human flesh!'

'No, no, no!' Jake cried. 'It was Karl. Karl is the vampire.'

'Karl is as human as you or I,' Sandor said.

'He casts a shadow. We've seen him in the daytime. When have you ever seen Rebecca in the day? She only ever comes out at night!'

Jake wouldn't believe what he was hearing. He turned to Rebecca. But it was no longer the Rebecca he knew. Her normally dark and narrow eyes were now wide and red, and her mouth was drawn back to reveal her flawlessly white teeth – and her two massive and hungry fangs. She hissed at Jake.

And then Jake realised that Sandor and Vicky were right: that he had never seen Rebecca during the day, how she had refused a mirror when he had offered her one. He remembered the night he had first gone to Hobb Hill, and she had watched him from her turret window. Rebecca told him that she hadn't called out because Karl was in the room with her, but Karl had been outside and had warned Jake to stay away from his 'sister'.

Jake tried to take a step back, but Rebecca's grip on his hand was too strong.

'You belong to me now, Jake,' she spat. 'You with your rare blood group, that same blood that once ran in my veins. To drink of your blood shall be a champagne feast!'

She grabbed Jake's neck and plunged her teeth towards his flesh. Sandor leapt forwards, trying to drag her off his best friend, but Rebecca was too strong for him, too strong for anyone. With an angry roar she threw Sandor aside, as someone might a rag doll. He cracked his head on the floor and passed out.

Jake struggled in the arms of the girl he loved, trying desperately to free himself from her deadly embrace. The skin of his neck wasn't yet punctured, and Rebecca brought her mouth down once more for her deadly kiss.

Crash!

Rebecca snarled, and released Jake. As he fell to the floor, he saw one of the walls of the set explode in a shower of splinters, just as it had done in his dream of the other night. Karl shot through the wall on his motorbike, and landed several feet away from them. His eyes darted this way and that, quickly taking in the scene before him.

Rebecca laughed in his face. 'So, dear brother, you've found me,' she growled. 'What are you going to do now? I know that neither you nor my beloved sister' – she glanced back at the old woman – 'will kill me.'

'We love you, Rebecca,' Karl said, and Jake was surprised to hear a touch of sadness and regret in the punk's voice for the first time. 'That is why my grandmother and I have stayed with you all these years. That is why I broke into Jake's lab last night. If we could have found a suitable blood substitute, there would have been an end to all your killing.'

But love no longer meant anything to Rebecca. She glanced at Jake, lying semiconscious on the floor. She licked her lips. Kim's and Sara's blood had been weak and tasteless: it had been like drinking vinegar. Such poor fare angered her, which was why she had savaged their bodies after she had drunk her fill. But Jake, with that rich, rare blood flowing through his veins, would be a feast indeed. She moved towards him.

Vicky looked at the old woman, who was regarding the scene with a strange passivity. *She's seen this before!* Vicky suddenly realised. *She's seen it time and time again over the years!*

'We must do something!' Vicky pleaded with her. By now Rebecca was almost upon Jake's prone figure.

'The fire extinguisher,' the old woman said, nodding towards the old-fashioned extinguisher near one of the cameras. It was marked: *Not for use on electrical fires.*

'What?'

'Vampires may not cross running water!' the old woman told her. 'Now use it!'

Vicky ran over to the extinguisher and aimed a stream of water between Rebecca and Jake, cutting the vampire off from her intended prey. Rebecca leapt back in anger and surprise, just as if she had been scalded. She turned to Rebecca, her eyes blazing with hatred.

'If I can't have Jake, then I will have you!' she said, rushing at Vicky. Vicky aimed the fire extinguisher directly at Rebecca. She fell back once again, screaming in agony. Vicky came closer to Rebecca's writhing body, turning the full force of the water on her.

And then the water failed. Vicky dropped the empty extinguisher to the ground and looked around for another, but the only ones she could see used carbon-dioxide and not water. Somehow she thought that CO_2 would not have the same effect on a vampire as pure running H_2O.

Rebecca pulled herself up from the ground. Her chest was steaming, where the water had hit her. She stalked towards Vicky. 'You have caused me pain,' she said. 'Now you die!'

'Rebecca?'

Rebecca turned to see Jake, who had regained consciousness and was struggling to his feet. She licked her lips again.

'You lied to me, Rebecca,' Jake sobbed. 'You said you loved me.'

Rebecca laughed scornfully. 'Loved you?' she scoffed. 'I have loved many men since I died in the 1940s. You were but the latest in a long line of lovers, lovers whose kisses were dry but whose blood was sweeter than wine.'

'I loved you,' Jake said, and now the tears were streaming down his face. 'And deep down inside, I think I always will.'

Rebecca laughed again. Such pitiful emotions were for fools!

'And it's because I love you, that I'm doing this.'

'Jake?' Rebecca said, and then screamed. 'Jake, please, don't!'

Jake had taken a large shard of wood from the splintered scenery. He threw himself at the girl he loved, and in one swift and brutal motion drove the wooden spike through her false heart.

Jake lay for long moments on top of Rebecca's now motionless body, weeping. Finally he felt a pair of hands lift him up. It was Karl, and when Jake looked at the young punk's face, he saw that he had been sobbing too.

'She is dead now, Jake,' Karl said. 'Truly dead. After over fifty years of being a vampire, she has finally found peace.' He cradled Jake's head in his shoulder, like a mother might a crying baby. 'Neither her sister – my grandmother – nor I could bring ourselves to kill her. In the end it seems that you loved her much more than we did.'

Through misty eyes, Jake looked down at the body of Rebecca, her heart punctured by the stake he had driven through it. Her eyes were closed and there was a beatific smile on her face.

But it was not the face of the girl he had loved. This face was much older, with lines around the eyes and mouth, and the hair completely grey. It was the face of Rebecca at her true age.

Jake looked over at the old woman from the house on Hobb Hill. She was tending Sandor, who was rapidly regaining consciousness. Jake nodded wisely to himself: yes, now he could see the family resemblance.

Through misty eyes Jake looked down at
the body of Elsie on the bunk, murdered by
the knife he had driven through her. Her eyes
were closed and there was a restful smile on
her face.

But it was not the face of the girl he had
loved. This face was small-eyed, with nose
round, the eyes and mouth, and the chin
completely gray. It was the face of Rebecca in
their late age.

Jake looked over at the old woman it was
her face on Trinh, till he was coming.
Sundown, who was rapidly resuming consciousness, had pulled away to himself,
may now he would use the facility a sear-
mad to...

Chapter Twelve

It had been a good year, Jake decided, as he ran the hot water for his evening bath. He squeezed some shaving cream on to his hand and rubbed it into the bristles of his beard.

Twelve months after Rebecca's death, he was going out with a really cute girl, so sexy that even Sandor was jealous of him. The charges against his best friend had been dropped when the old lady from the house on Hobb Hill had produced vital evidence which seemed to point to her grandson, Karl Vondertoten, as being guilty of the murders of Kim and Sara, and of another, unidentified old woman found in the back lot of a film studio.

Karl, however, had somehow eluded the police and escaped justice. No one knew where he was. Well, no one, Jake reflected, apart from himself and Sandor, Vicky and the old woman herself, and they certainly weren't going to tell Detective Sergeant Ashby or any of his colleagues.

Karl had turned out to be an OK guy after all, Jake decided, as he started shaving. Sure, he had a bit of an attitude problem and he and Jake would never be best mates, but his heart was in the right place.

Vicky, who had taken something of a shine to him, even said that he was a bit of a softie and a real sensitive soul. Karl had told her about the time when he had taken Rebecca home across the Heath, and she had attacked and slaughtered Kim. When he had seen Kim's corpse, he had thrown up there and then, right beside the body.

What a wimp! Jake thought. *As if seeing a gutted and steaming human carcass was enough to make someone throw up! Some guys just didn't have the stomach!*

Jake finished shaving and wiped his face clean with a hand-towel. He was already looking forward to his date tonight. His new girlfriend was really hot stuff, and a great kisser. Although not as good as Rebecca, he decided: Rebecca sure knew how to kiss!

As he hung the towel on the rail, he noticed a fleck of blood on it.

Damn! he thought. *Don't say I've cut myself shaving again!* He rubbed his hand across his chin: sure enough, he was bleeding.

Lately this was happening far too often, he realised. But what could he do? He always shaved as carefully as possible, but without a shaving mirror these little nicks and scratches were bound to happen.

Jake had no need of shaving mirrors. Three months ago – nine months after Rebecca had kissed him on the film lot – he had thrown all his mirrors away.

After all, to use a mirror it does help if you have a reflection, doesn't it?

NEW BOOKS FROM

B▨XTREE

ZOOL

MEET ZOOL, THE ALIEN NINJA FROM THE NTH DIMENSION

'Cooler than Mario, smarter than Sonic . . .'

Two things Zool is not!
1. Boring . . .
2. An ant. This is a vile lie put about by his arch enemy Mental Block. Ants are small, hard working insects with lots of legs, Zool is an alien from outer space with breath-taking powers. Also ants do not have their names written on the soles of their shoes. And Zool does, so there!

ZOOL RULES
Isbn: 0 7522 0952 3

Coming soon:
COOL ZOOL
Isbn: 0 7522 0957 4

MIGHTY MORPHIN POWER RANGERS

The Mighty Morphin Power Rangers are teenagers with special abilities brought together to defend the Earth against an intergalactic sorceress named Rita. Drawing strength from the spirits of ancient dinosaurs, the Rangers also benefit from the futuristic technology given to them by the inter-dimensional being, Zordon.

IT'S MORPHIN TIME!
Isbn: 0 7522 0939 6

MEGAZORD TO THE RESCUE!
Isbn: 0 7522 0944 2

THE TERROR TOAD
Isbn: 0 7522 0949 3

RITA'S REVENGE
Isbn: 0 7522 0954 X

TAKE THAT

Introducing the books every
Take That fan should read!

TAKE THAT –
OUR STORY

Piers Morgan

The hottest band in Britain are talented, down-to-earth, funny and hard working. Now, for the first time, the boys have told their own amazing story.

Isbn: 1 85283 839 6

TAKE THAT ON THE ROAD

Piers Morgan

Take That have taken the charts by storm and driven teenage girls mad all over the world with their fresh-faced good looks and slick dance routines. This book takes a behind-the-scenes look at Take That on tour and gives an insight into this incredibly popular band.

Isbn: 1 85283 396 3

TAKE THAT UNDER MY PILLOW

This gift pack of five mini books in a slipcase is essential reading for any Take That fan. Each book is devoted to one of the stars of the band and contains twenty exclusive photographs with their fact files and quotes.

Isbn: 0 7522 0988 4

SAVED BY THE BELL

This hit US teen show follows the inventive schemes and mischievous dreams of Bayside High's wacky students. Now on Channel Four Television, Saved By The Bell looks set to become as popular in the UK as it has been in the States.

Novelisations:

ZACK'S LAST SCAM
Isbn: 0 7522 0990 6

ZACK STRIKES BACK
Isbn: 0 7522 0985 X

GIRLS' NIGHT OUT
Isbn: 0 7522 0901 9

ONE WILD WEEKEND
Isbn: 0 7522 0955 7

SUPER SAVED BY THE BELL SCRAPBOOK
Isbn: 0 7522 0961 2

CALIFORNIA DREAMS

The hit TV teen show, California Dreams, has been described as a cross between *Beverly Hills 90210* and *The Monkees*. Superhunk, Jake, and his high school friends form a rock band called . . . California Dreams.

Novelisations:
PLAYING FOR KEEPS
Isbn: 0 7522 0916 7

PERFECT HARMONY
Isbn: 0 7522 0906 X

WHO CAN YOU TRUST?
Isbn: 0 7522 0911 6

HOW TO ORDER YOUR BOXTREE BOOKS

HORROR HIGH

☐ 0 7522 0996 3	*Bad Moon Rising*	£2.99
☐ 0 7522 0971 X	*Rave On!*	£2.99
☐ 1 85283 358 0	*Symphony of Terror*	£2.99
☐ 1 85283 363 7	*Demon Brood*	£2.99

ZOOL

☐ 0 7522 0952 3	*Zool Rules*	£3.99
☐ 0 7522 0957 4	*Cool Zool*	£3.99

MIGHTY MORPHIN POWER RANGERS

☐ 0 7522 0939 6	*It's Morphin Time*	£2.99
☐ 0 7522 0944 2	*Megazord To The Rescue*	£2.99
☐ 0 7522 0949 3	*The Terror Toad*	£2.99
☐ 0 7522 0954 X	*Rita's Revenge*	£2.99

TAKE THAT

☐ 1 85283 839 6	*Our Story*	£5.99
☐ 1 85283 396 3	*On The Road*	£5.99
☐ 0 7522 0988 4	*Under My Pillow*	£5.99

SAVED BY THE BELL

☐ 0 7522 0990 6	*Zack's Last Scam*	£3.50
☐ 0 7522 0985 X	*Zack Strikes Back*	£3.50
☐ 0 7522 0901 9	*Girls' Night Out*	£3.50
☐ 0 7522 0955 7	*One Wild Weekend*	£3.50
☐ 0 7522 0961 2	*Super Saved By The Bell Scrapbook*	£3.99

CALIFORNIA DREAMS

☐ 0 7522 0916 7	*Playing For Keeps*	£3.50
☐ 0 7522 0906 X	*Perfect Harmony*	£3.50
☐ 0 7522 0911 6	*Who Can You Trust?*	£3.50

All these books are available at your local bookshop or newsagent, or can be ordered direct from the publisher. Just tick the titles you want and fill in the form below.

Prices and availability subject to charge without notice.

Boxtree Cash Sales, P.O. Box 11, Falmouth, Cornwall TR10 9EN

Please send a cheque or postal order for the value of the book and add the following for postage and packing:

U.K. including B.F.P.O. – £1.00 for one book plus 50p for the second book, and 30p for each additional book ordered up to a £3.00 maximum.

Overseas including Eire – £2.00 for the first book plus £1.00 for the second book, and 50p for each additional book ordered.

OR please debit this amount from my Access/Visa Card (delete as appropriate).

Card Number 1 6 4 0 1 6 0 1 0 7 7

Amount £ 10

Expiry Date on card

Signed Liam

Name LIAM

Address Llyppe brighton road